BORN EVIL

BOOK ONE IN THE EVIL TRILOGY

JULIA DEREK

ADRENALINE BOOKS

For the person in my life who I hope will come to his senses soon.

1

Macy, the cat, was already dead by the time I could tell what was going on inside the living room. Shane had already managed to kill the poor animal. My first instinct had been to run inside the country house and make my twelve-year-old son stop stabbing Macy when I spotted them through the windows. But when I realized that the cat was partially *decapitated,* I stayed put on the lawn outside; it was too late. No matter what I did, sweet Macy would never purr again.

Every single one of her nine lives had been spent.

Shane himself was so fixated on what he had done, the mess he had created before him on the pale wooden floor, that he didn't notice me standing right outside the living-room windows and gazing inside. Only a few yards separated us, yet it felt like I was looking into a separate universe, light years away. At least for part of me. The other part wasn't as shocked.

Deep inside I had always feared something like this would happen eventually.

I don't know how long I remained outside in the darkness, staring at all the blood around the furry body on the living-room floor. It looked black and thick like oil against the blond floorboards. It could have been for just a second or it could have been for several. All I know is that, at some point, I bent over and threw up on the lawn. Or tried to throw up, as much didn't come out of me. Mostly, I heaved quietly. It had been hours since I'd eaten anything but that apple on my way over to Beth's.

Once I finished retching, I forced myself back up into an upright position. The scene in the living room right before me had changed. Instead of stabbing a bread knife over and over into the poor cat, my son was now on his knees, busy cleaning up the mess on the floor. He had brought a bucket of water, a spray bottle of Clorox All Purpose Cleaner, and a fresh roll of paper towels. It dawned on me that I should be grateful dusk had fallen nearly half an hour ago. It was so dark outside that it was extremely unlikely Shane had discovered he'd had an audience for his heinous deed. Even if he turned his head and glanced out at the small lawn, he wasn't bound to see me standing in the middle of it. Even so, I moved away from that spot and leaned my back against the brown wooden wall of my parents' one-story country house. I needed some time to pull myself together, figure out what to do.

Calm down, Jennifer, I ordered myself. *You freaking out about this won't do anyone any good. Now you know for sure.*

Deal with it. He's still your son. Remember, it can be fixed. The developments reversed. You'll just have to try harder. Besides, it's all your fault it's happening anyway.

I closed my eyes and wiped my mouth dry with the back of my hand, then licked my lips. I swallowed hard in a futile attempt to get rid of the bitter taste of bile, but it only made it worse. I took a few deep breaths to settle down and reminded myself that at least my son, bad or not, was alive, unlike Beth's niece; she'd recently fallen to her death from a cliff. Beth was still in pieces about it, almost as much as her sister, the girl's mother, which was why I had gone over to her house tonight. Tonight had been the four-month anniversary of Alice's death, so she could use the company. Shane had wanted to keep playing video games, so I'd left him at home. He was old and mature enough to be alone for the evening. He could always call me and I was only a couple of miles away. It would be easier to console Beth without him around anyway.

You'll fix this, Jennifer, I kept telling myself. *You fix everything. You'll find a way to make him normal again. You have to. It's your fault he's this way. You should have protected him better. He doesn't deserve spending his life in an institution.*

I needed to get away for a while so Shane could take care of what he had done. Hide all the traces. I instinctively knew that he was going to want to hide it one way or another, and for that to happen, I needed to give him time. I needed to give him several minutes, a couple of hours even. He wasn't expecting me home until much later anyway. Barging into the house now would screw with his plan. His reckless, reckless plan.

Recklessness. Another trademark of the psychopathic mind.

I opened my eyes and suddenly noticed the faint sound of music in the air. In the immense stillness of the countryside where even the bush-crickets were quiet at the moment, it was almost jarring. Had it been there all along? I couldn't be sure. Where did it come from? From my current vantage point, I could tell that the TV was on in the living room. I couldn't see much, only that the screen was bright and what looked like people were dancing around on it. The music must come from the TV then.

Feeling like a zombie, I walked over to where I'd parked my car, a red Honda Civic, about eight yards away. I couldn't stay here. Halfway to the car, I froze; it had struck me that Shane must have heard me drive onto the gravel-covered driveway. He usually did. Fear shot through me, wrapping itself around my throat like a snake, which made it hard to breathe. Had he *wanted* me to witness him stabbing Macy to death? Oh God, he must have... Why *else* had he kept stabbing the cat in front of me? My heart punched against my ribs like an infuriated wild bird trapped in a small cage. Wait. I was overreacting. He probably hadn't heard me. The TV was on in the living room, and he'd clearly jacked up the volume the way he always did when I wasn't around to tell him to keep it down. If I concentrated hard, I could still hear the music. Yes, the loud sound must have drowned out the engine's soft roaring. The stifling panic slowly uncurled itself from around my windpipe and I relaxed my shoulders.

That meant he wouldn't hear when I drove off either, I told myself and hurried over to the car. I snuck into the driver's seat and tried to stick the key into the ignition. I fumbled and nearly dropped the keys, but at long last I managed to get the correct one inside the slot. Tossing a tentative glance at the dark country house several yards behind me, I turned the key and the engine came alive, rumbling steadily. Carefully, I pulled out of the uneven driveway and onto the dirt road and took off. Thankfully, I could still make out the edges of every object around me, so I left the car lights unlit. I didn't dare turn them on until I was further down the road where Shane wouldn't be able to see me.

Soon, even the house's silhouette was no longer visible in the rearview mirror, so I switched on the lights. Pressing down the gas pedal, I picked up the pace now that I could see well. I knew I wouldn't return for a while.

I wouldn't return until I had figured out how to deal with the fact that my son had finally turned into the psychopath I had feared him becoming for so long.

2

I can see the old Shane whenever I want to. All I need to do is close my eyes and focus a bit. It's not hard at all. Old Shane is really very young Shane, because the sweet little boy I see in my mind's eye is only three years old. It's a three-year-old with a tousled head of blond hair so light it's almost white, and round, red cheeks that everyone wants to pinch. There are freckles around the little nose and a front tooth has grown in slightly crooked, a fact displayed proudly each time he smiles. The teal-colored eyes are surrounded by long, dark lashes and gaze at you with that serious curiosity only children can pull off.

Shane was adorable at that age, like a little angel.

By age six, his hair had darkened and the crooked baby tooth was gone, an adult one about to take its place.

It was in his sixth year that the unthinkable was revealed to me and his father, Peter. The unthinkable that we, being his parents, should have prevented from ever happening. As his mother, I felt especially responsible. I should have protected him from the abuse. I should have known, deep down in my gut, that having Peter's big brother Tony babysit our child was a bad, bad idea. The guy wasn't as squeaky clean and normal as he pretended to be. Anyone could see that. Besides, weren't mothers supposed to have this sixth sense when it came to their children that helped shield them from all that's evil in the world?

Well, if that was so, I wasn't one of those mothers. Which was particularly strange as I was definitely one of those people who were good at reading others. At least I was now. I suppose back then, several years earlier when I was in my twenties and less confident, I simply didn't trust my talent enough. Sadly, there were still times that I didn't.

I suppose the fact that I myself was sexually abused when I was a little girl has something to do with it. By my seven-year-older brother, Nick. I haven't told anyone about that, not even my own parents. What's the point? It won't change anything and my brother is dead now anyway. He got what he deserved in a bar brawl. Puny Nick was beaten to death by another, much bigger guy for behaving badly toward his girlfriend. The couple got away and no one has seen them since that fateful night. Yes, my mother and father don't need to know the truth about Nick. It would only upset them.

Neither Peter nor I realized that his sick brother had systematically abused our only child for over a year in the worst possible way. The harm had already been done when we found out. Shane had been put through unspeakable trauma at the hands of his uncle. I would discover later on that this trauma had likely unleashed the psychopathic tendencies Shane was born with. According to the mental health professionals I spoke with, little could be done to reverse those tendencies once they had been let out. Naturally, I never told these people why I had wanted to know about the mechanics of the mind. The day Peter and I were told of our child's abnormal brain and genetic alleles, mere days after his third birthday, we'd promised each other that we would keep it a secret to the world. We had stumbled upon his psychopathically inclined brain after having it checked for damages after a minor concussion, using PET scanning.

After all, the doctor had assured us that, as long as we kept showering Shane with love like we'd been doing since the day he was born, he would be fine. We had nothing to worry about. Shane also needed structure and good role models to develop into a functioning individual. Scientific studies had proven over and over that nurture was stronger than nature in cases like these.

So, to squelch his mind's criminal inclinations from the get-go, we loved our little boy more than ever and went out of our way to provide a stable environment. It seemed to work because he was generally high-spirited, fun and friendly, not to mention bright. An enviable child. I stayed home taking care of him, while Peter worked full-time as the in-house accountant for a hospital. Once a week we had date night, and that was when Tony babysat Shane.

Given all the time I was around my son, I will never forgive myself for failing to put two and two together, never realizing exactly why he began acting out and becoming more boisterous. At the time, when Shane had turned five, Peter and I assumed he was going through a phase; even Shane's pediatrician thought so. I had begun to write on a screenplay while Shane was in kindergarten, so I also saw less of him than before. I had always dreamed of becoming an actress, flirted with it as a career even, but then I got pregnant and had to give up those dreams. The bug never got out of me, though, and I loved play-acting whenever I got the chance. I was a big fan of method acting, which I was introduced to while taking classes at the Lee Strasberg Film & Theatre Institute. Method acting is when you become the character you play, emotionally as well as physically. Once, when Shane was four, I stayed in character for days while play-acting at home. When I realized just how much it confused my son and husband, I stopped and started writing instead, pretending to be different characters in my head only. Soon I began writing screenplays. It was a good substitute for the acting, a way for me to feel like I was still part of the glamorous world of Hollywood movies. Maybe one day I would sell a screenplay. I secretly hoped so.

My project, a story about a transsexual boy growing up in a conservative home, absorbed me more than it should have, and I spent lots of time playing the different parts in my head. Like before, I fully immersed myself in the roles, becoming the person. Being in the head of each part helped me write better, more honestly. I thought I had reached the perfect middle ground making myself a happy, responsible stay-at-home mom, but clearly I hadn't. I simply didn't pay as much attention to my son's well-being as I should have. I deeply regret having gone after screenwriting with such vigor. Naturally, the screenplay went into the trash after I found out what Shane had been through. Never again would I do something so stupid, so frivolous when it took focus away from my child. Every day I beat myself up about my selfish acts, dreaming about a way to turn back time, undo what I had done.

Maybe if I had paid more attention, I would have caught on to what was happening to my son and been able to reverse the effects. The terrible effects that would eventually reveal themselves.

As soon as we found out about Shane's psychopathic inclinations, we decided not to have another child. We didn't want to risk giving birth to another with the same genes. Somewhere down our family lines, these genes lingered, and we were determined to stop giving them life. It was enough that Shane had gotten them, and judging from his behavior, arguably, so had Tony.

Instead of trying for another kid, we looked into adoption.

Adopting a child was not as easy as we had thought, though. By the time Shane had turned six, we had yet to get another child in our house. We were much closer, but when we finally got the news that we would get a small daughter from Russia, another family tragedy happened.

One so huge I have nightmares about it most days and am forced to take anti-anxiety pills to be able to fall sleep in the first place.

Shortly after we learned that Peter's brother had sexually abused our son—in a letter he had written after taking his own life by hanging himself—my husband died in an accident. Well, this is what everyone else in the world thought it was—an accident. Really, it was Shane's fault that Peter died and I'm not sure it was actually an accident. Shane was the one who'd pulled the trigger on the handgun Peter kept in a safe box.

To this day, I'm still wondering how Shane managed to get the safe box open, because I refuse to believe Peter had been so careless he forgot to lock it.

Just like I had caught my son coldly stabbing our cat to death, I had witnessed when he executed his own father by aiming a gun to his head. The Saturday it happened I had been about to enter the bedroom where Peter was taking a nap in the middle of the day. I didn't understand what Shane was doing when he walked up to Peter lying on the bed and pointed the gun; it was too bright in the room from all the sunshine bursting through the big windows. By the time I realized he held my husband's gun in his small hands, it was too late. Shane had already pulled the trigger.

As if in a foggy nightmare, I ran up to him. The gun had fallen out of his hands and lay next to his small feet. He remained in place five feet away from his father, calmly regarding his deed. He had hit Peter in the forehead, bright red blood seeping out from the round wound.

Judging from my husband's reaction, his body jerking, then collapsing on the bed, I instinctively knew he was dead.

But that hadn't been the worst part. The worst part had been the smile that spread over my son's lips and the words that came out of his mouth as I reached him.

"I told Daddy to let me have the ice cream when I wanted it," he stated in a flat voice. "If only he had listened, I wouldn't have had to punish him."

Right before lunch earlier that day, Peter had ordered Shane to put back the chocolate ice cream he had gotten from the fridge. "You know you're not supposed to eat ice cream before a meal, Shane. If you're a good boy and finish your vegetables, you can have some ice cream for dessert. Okay?"

Peter had ruffled Shane's thick mop of hair and only gotten a pout in return.

Numb with pain, I had let go of Shane and thrown myself over Peter, shaking him in a vain attempt to bring him back to life. Tears streaming down my face, I begged him to look at me and talk to me, tell me he was still with me. But nothing like that happened and eventually I was forced to stop and instead call the emergency services.

As I waited for the authorities and the ambulance to arrive, I turned to Shane, demanding to know how he had gotten hold of the gun. He told me the gun safe had been unlocked when he found it on a shelf in the walk-in closet.

"But why did you go to check in the first place?" I'd asked between sobs. "You *know* you're not supposed to be touching Daddy's gun!"

Shane looked at me with glassy eyes and sincerely stated, "He needed to be taught a lesson."

3

When help arrived, paramedics and police entering our house, I had convinced myself that I had only imagined my son smiling and telling me he'd needed to teach his dad a lesson. *Of course* I had. Shane would never say something like that, never do something like that on purpose. He was a good boy. It had just been an accident. Peter had forgotten to lock the gun safe after going to practice at the gun range earlier in the day, and this was what had happened.

Yes, it was horrible, but nonetheless the only explanation. It had all been a terrible, terrible accident. It had to be. I wouldn't accept anything else. My son was not a sick person.

It was exactly what I told the police when they asked me to explain what had happened: My son had found the gun and, not understanding it was a real one, used it to play with the way he did with his toy guns, pretending to shoot his father. He hadn't understood what he was doing. The boy was not even seven years old yet. How could he?

Much to my relief, everyone bought this explanation, even the child psychologist I had Shane see later. If the psychologist had knowledge of Shane's brain PET scan, he might've felt differently. I conveniently forgot about it, though. My son was so good at manipulating people even at that young age that he had everyone fooled, including his mother. Well, almost. Somewhere deep, deep inside I knew I was lying to myself, but I refused to let the truth into my conscious mind for several years. I didn't want to have my son committed. Not when it was his parents' own fault that he had turned into this monster. My fault in particular. I had to cure him, reverse the effects before they became permanent inside him. There was still time.

Peter had paid for not catching on to what his brother was doing to his son with his life. I had paid for it by witnessing my son execute his father and my husband. I had to at least try to cure Shane from the evil that was growing inside him. I refused to believe the doctors who'd told me the mental condition was irreversible once triggered. For God's sake, Shane was only a child! He was nowhere near fully developed. How could it be irreversible so early on? I didn't buy it. There had to be *something* I could do. So I started taking classes in psychology, in particular ones that involved the development of psychopathy.

I would find a way to fix my son, put him back on the right path. Kill whatever tendencies the sexual abuse had awakened inside him. If the mental health professionals didn't want to do it, I had no choice but to give it a go myself.

Of course, I didn't actually admit out loud that this was the reason I went back to school. Instead, I kept telling myself and others that I would become a social worker. Now that I was a widow, I wanted to have a real job even though the money Peter left us together with his life insurance was enough for me and Shane to live on if we lived frugally. Still, I would take my Master's degree in psychology as it only took two years of studies. I could make it happen even quicker if I took extra classes during the summer.

I would focus on education and research in the field of psychopathy, not actually work with clients. I could always get a job in the field later in life if I needed to.

I used everything I learned to encourage my son to become a functioning adult; instill in him the difference between right and wrong. I would turn him into a good person. Not necessarily one with much empathy for others, as, apparently, he wasn't capable of such feelings. That wasn't my goal, though. As long as he did the right thing and never hurt anyone or anything else ever again, I was satisfied. Hurt anyone on purpose, that is.

According to what I had learned, that was as good as it got for people with brains like Shane's who'd been through traumatic events.

I thought I was succeeding until that night in late August at my parents' country house in upstate New York.

That look on my son's face, the fired-up glint in his eyes

as he'd viciously stabbed our poor cat, had been enough to convince me all my efforts had been in vain. None of it had worked. It was as though he'd been dealing with a crazed lion, not a sweet house cat.

I kept driving along the dark dirt road, switching on the car lights when I was much farther ahead. The moon was almost full and shining from a charcoal sky full of stars that kept igniting as night fell over the peaceful countryside.

I didn't know where I was heading; I just kept gripping the steering wheel like I feared I would lose it if I let go. Going back to Beth was not an option. I was dying to share what had happened with her, one of my very best friends. It was not an option, however. I couldn't trust her not to tell others what Shane had done. The only way to keep his condition a secret was if no one ever found out about it. I needed to think, decide what to do. How to best protect both Shane and the world around him from him.

Was it possible that I was overreacting? Or wait, that I had misunderstood what had been going on in the living room? Oh, if only that was so! No, I really didn't think I had misunderstood anything. I had barely drunk half a glass of wine and it had been very easy for me to make out what was going on inside the house. I had been only yards away, for crying out loud. Still, the fact that Shane had been stabbing a cat, not a human, had to be taken into consideration, I told myself. While the act was terrible, it wasn't quite as bad as it could have been, was it? I mean, it *could* have been a human being... That would have been so much worse. Really, it would. I also needed to take into account the fact that he hadn't done anything that could be considered psychopathic since the day he had shot Peter, more than six years ago.

Believe me, I had been watching him closely ever since.

Yes, I suddenly decided. It was possible I was overreacting just a little. The situation wasn't as bad as it had first seemed. Thank God I hadn't gone back to Beth and poured my heart out to her.

I stepped on the gas pedal and drove faster along the winding country road. So far, I hadn't bumped into a single car. That would change when I reached the main road that was quickly approaching. I could drive even faster on that road as it was covered with newly laid asphalt, smooth like a baby's butt, and the lanes much wider and straighter. The car would no longer shiver and shake as I drove over stones and potholes of varying size and shape.

Five minutes later, when a single car had met me, I reached the main road and took a right onto it. I would allow myself to relax and let my intuition guide me in terms of how to tackle this situation. My intuition was strong and good, helping me choose the best approach to life. I was confident it would lead me on the right path this time, too.

4

I declined the offer to adopt a two-year-old girl from Russia. The offer came the day before Peter's funeral, which had been on a Friday. There was no way I'd be able to raise another child after what had happened. I wasn't even sure I'd be able to raise Shane properly, I had been so beyond myself with grief. All I wanted to do was lie down on a bed and stare into the ceiling, pretend I was dead like Peter. Forget about all the horror that was my life. But I couldn't do that. I couldn't just check out. I had another person who depended on me. Peter and I had already failed our son once; no matter what he had done, I needed to stand by him, take care of him. What had happened wasn't really his fault. I could never allow myself to forget that.

The thought of what would happen to Shane if I didn't pull myself together was what kept me going those days. I needed to stay stronger than ever for my son, our son. I couldn't resort to drowning myself in an alcoholic daze, nor stuffing myself full with painkillers and anxiety-mini-mizing meds. It was bad enough that I had to take the meds to be able to fall, not to mention stay asleep.

My head needed to be clear for Shane's sake. I had to help him back onto the right path. He hadn't meant to kill his father. It had been a temporary lapse, likely a belated reaction to what Tony had put him through. He had been acting out all his pent-up frustration, which was completely understandable. If Peter and I had found him the right therapist sooner, it would probably never have happened at all, and I would see to it that it never happened again.

It seemed I was correct in my assumption. Shane's behavior the morning after he'd shot his father helped to convince me all was good. Shane was no longer silent, staring into the distance with eyes that were disturbingly flat. Instead, when he asked for Peter and I told him he was dead, he had burst out in tears and been incon-solable for hours. He had cried so hard I regretted telling him the truth; a white lie would have been better. A white lie to protect him. At the time, I had figured that, if he could handle getting hold of his father's gun and shooting him, he could also handle the truth. Apparently, it had been harder for him to deal with it than I had anticipated, which was a relief. It showed me that I had been right. It had all just been an awful accident. I didn't have to worry about having lied to the police, I told myself and exhaled. Shane had had no idea what he'd been doing.

I even told the police that my husband had forgotten to

lock the gun storage box, as well as removing the chair from the closet. That had to be the case, I convinced myself. How else would Shane have been able to get the gun from that shelf? The idea that the boy had brought the chair himself was simply preposterous. Right?

Peter and I had been on the lookout for the right child therapist ever since we learned what Tony had done to Shane. Our regular doctor had recommended that we went about life as usual not to upset Shane more than he already was. What was done could not be undone anyway, only treated.

We'd taken our son to two different psychologists so far, and the second was worse than the first. Dr. Whitehead, who'd seemed promising in the beginning, had fallen asleep during the second session. He had been sleeping so soundly that it had taken Peter several hard knocks on his office door to bring him back to reality. The second psychologist, a social worker named Rachel Gordon who specialized in traumatized children, had been far too aggressive, to the point that she had left Shane in tears that lasted long after every session was over. After the third session, neither Peter nor I had felt that we should stick with Ms. Gordon. In fact, after his short acquaintance with the second therapist, we'd mistakenly decided that Shane needed a break from therapy in general.

Unfortunately, beating myself up about this stupid decision led to nothing, so I had just sucked it up and found a third therapist once I was strong enough to hold myself together enough to face the world.

I was keeping my fingers crossed that Dr. Handelburg, a

psychiatrist who'd worked with sexually abused children, would work out better for Shane.

It looked like I was in luck because the sixty-year-old German-born doctor and Shane had instantly clicked.

"I do believe your son wasn't aware of what he was doing when he shot his father," the white-haired man informed me after the initial two-hour session was over. "He was just playing. He had no idea he was dealing with a real gun that could kill people." I had decided that we would do a long initial session instead of having him go for short ones once a week, something the pediatrician had thought was better as well. Given the fact that the authorities wanted a mental health professional to talk to Shane as soon as possible, I'd really had no choice but to switch approaches. As long as I could find a reputable psychiatrist, a mental health professional the police's own people approved of, to vouch for my son's mental state, we were good.

Relief mixed with happiness streamed through my veins as I heard Dr. Handelburg's verdict. "Really?" I asked, feeling my eyes filling up with warm tears of gratitude. I blinked them away as I needed to remain composed. But it was too late, the kind doctor had already noticed my state of mind. He placed a veiny hand on my arm and gave a small, toothless smile.

"And when are you going to see a therapist, Ms. Hanson?" he asked soothingly. "You need to see someone as much as your son does in order to deal with the grief. This has been as trying for you as it's been for your son. More so, I dare venture."

I allowed a few of the tears to meander down my cheeks and returned his smile. He was so right; I, too, needed to talk to someone. I was dangerously near a nervous breakdown. If I wanted to stay strong for my son, I needed to take care of myself in every sense of that word.

"Yes, you're right, Dr. Handelburg," I said. "Do you recommend someone for me?"

He nodded and went behind his desk where he pulled out a drawer. When his hand returned, there was a business card in it that he gave me.

"I think Dr. Wilkins will be a good fit for you. Call him."

"I will," I said. "Thank you."

5

___

It was almost eleven at night and pitch-black outside when I decided to return to the country house and Shane. I had spent over two hours driving mindlessly on the roads in the area, replaying what had happened in our living room. Praying that I had somehow been mistaken after all, seeing someone else other than my son repeatedly stabbing Macy. An intruder, another child. Anyone would do, even the neighbor's teenage son, who was small for his age. He and Shane were roughly the same size and had the same coloring, wore the same type of clothes.

But I knew that was all wishful thinking. There was nothing wrong with my eyesight and I had not been under the influence. It had been Shane and no one else that I'd seen. Oh God.

When I'd finally accepted this, I briefly pondered getting a weapon so I could defend myself when I returned home. That would be the smart thing to do, right? After what I had witnessed, I couldn't count on Shane not attacking me next with that big knife. What if he had completely snapped? Unfortunately, I thought this was very possible.

It was best if I was armed with at least a knife, I decided. The problem was that no stores were open at this late hour where I could buy one. Not up here in the woods. The closest one, a Walmart, was too far away. *Well,* I thought. I could drive back to Beth's house and get one from her. While waiting for a traffic light to turn green a couple of hours ago, I had texted Beth to tell her that Shane was sick and that I really had to stay with him. I'd make it up to her tomorrow. She'd texted back and offered to come over and help out, but I had assured her it was best she stayed home. She hadn't insisted, thank God.

No, before I confessed the truth to her, I needed to make sure it was really necessary to bring a knife. I didn't want to include her in this otherwise. To establish that, I had to speak to Shane first, feel him out.

I pulled over to the road's shoulder and stopped, then found my phone again. Taking a few deep breaths to steel myself, I called Shane's cell phone.

He picked up after two rings the way he usually did.

"Hi, Mom. What's up?" His voice was nowhere near as cheery as usual, though. He sounded scared and as though he was on guard. I could hear him breathe shallowly, albeit faintly. I was momentarily thrown. What was going on?

Quietly, I cleared my throat and forced myself to smile. "Hi, honey. I'll be coming home soon. I just wanted to see if you were up still. What are you doing? Everything okay?"

"I'm playing video games."

"Oh. I—"

"Mom."

"Yes, honey?"

"Macy attacked me. Like attacked me really bad. Something's *wrong* with Macy..."

"What? Macy attacked you? Attacked you how? Are you okay?" I struggled to sound concerned. All I could picture was Shane stabbing the poor cat over and over.

"I don't know! All of a sudden, she went all *crazy* and started to bite and scratch me like she had turned into a wild tiger. I had to take her out. I'm sorry, I know you love her so much, but it was the only way to get her to stop hurting me. I think she had rabies or something. She must have. It's the only explanation."

Closing my eyes for a moment, I pictured Shane stabbing Macy in my mind yet again. Was it possible that he was telling the truth? Had he only been *defending* himself all along? Defending himself and gotten carried away, he'd been so terrified by Macy's out of character behavior? I honestly couldn't be sure. I had been too disturbed by what I had witnessed to have bothered looking for scratches or bite marks anywhere on my son. All I could remember now was that he'd worn something light and short-sleeved—probably the same T-shirt he'd worn when I'd left the house—and baggy jeans that hung low on his bony hips. I decided that it was possible, maybe even likely. I'd know if Shane was telling the truth when I saw him, if he was full of marks. There had to be several all over him that I had missed in that case. A sense of gratitude filled me. Yes, I would know the truth when I saw Shane next. Already I felt certain it was like he'd claimed. He would hardly lie to me about something he couldn't fake, right? He knew very well that I'd take a close look at his skin as soon as I saw him. So he had to be telling me the truth then. I opened my eyes and exhaled with relief.

"Mom? Are you still there?"

"Yeah. I'm sorry, honey. I'm still in shock to hear that Macy *attacked* you," I said quickly. "Are you okay?"

"Yes. I managed to take her out before she could do any serious damage. It was horrible. It was like she refused to die, so I had to really come at her."

"Take... her out? What do you mean?"

"I had to kill her. With a knife that I got from the kitchen. I had no choice. I had to defend myself. I honestly thought she was going to *kill* me, Mom!" He sounded suddenly several years younger, his voice small and pleading. I felt better, even more convinced that this was what had really happened. Shane hadn't instigated anything, only defended himself. Macy had done something completely out of character due to rabies, viciously attacked him. I nodded to myself; it made sense. She'd always been a lively cat that liked to explore and play with other animals. She loved to be outside whenever we went upstate and, lately, she'd been out a lot. In fact, I hadn't seen much of her in the last few days. Some rabies-infested bat or raccoon could easily have bitten her. I distinctly remembered having read somewhere recently that the rabies-virus had returned to this part of the United States after over a hundred years of it being considered rabies-free. Several bats up in the Catskills where we were had been infected, which meant that other animals could've been infected as well. Yes, this was what had happened—Macy had developed rabies and turned into a monster. Why hadn't I thought of *that* until now?

Shane was suddenly crying in my ear. "I'm sorry, Mom. I was so scared...I thought she was gonna kill me..."

"Shhh. It's okay, honey. I'm coming home in a few minutes. Will you be okay until then?"

"Yes..." He hiccupped miserably. "Please come soon, Mom... I'm still so scared."

"I will, honey. I will. See you soon. Goodbye."

"Goodbye..."

I pulled back out onto the road and took off, remembering the reason I'd come up with for calling Shane in the first place. My plan had been to claim to need a phone number from a business card in my bedroom to give to Beth. I'd needed a valid reason to call so suddenly or Shane might get suspicious. I hated myself now for having thought such a thing about my own son. I should've figured there was an explanation to what he'd done! I shouldn't have jumped to conclusions like that. When I got home, which would be in ten minutes if I drove real fast, I would find all the scratch marks and bites on Shane. He couldn't make something like that up. He would never be able to explain away not having any marks, and he knew that. To be one hundred percent sure, I would have the cat checked for rabies. A veterinarian shouldn't have a problem checking that out for me.

I had to drive quickly or Shane would wonder why it took me so long to get back from Beth's house. I didn't want him to wonder, crying on his own about what he'd been forced to do to Macy.

It was in that moment I saw the deer before me on the road. The large animal, frozen in place, looked at me in mild surprise. I swerved hard to avoid hitting it. Then all I remembered was driving off the road followed by a wall of black.

6

"Mom? Mom? Can you hear me? Mom?"

Slowly, I opened my eyes. The lids felt heavy, like someone had attached something to them that weighed a lot. Everything around me was bright and blurry and white, and someone sat next to me, looking down at me. No, there were two people, one bigger than the other. I forced myself to blink a couple of times to be able to see better.

Shane sat there, and so did Beth. Both of them were smiling widely, excitedly.

"Mom!" Shane exclaimed and grabbed my hand with both of his. "You're back!"

"Hi, Jennifer," Beth said, also excited but in a more contained manner. Her long auburn hair was pulled back in a ponytail and she was wearing glasses instead of contacts. Black-framed ones that made her look like a different person. "We were so worried we had lost you."

I looked around the room. I was in a squeaky clean hospital room, everything crispy white or shiny metallic, machines beeping and blinking. There was a window with the thick blinds drawn and shut on one side. An IV drip was attached to my hand on the side of the bed where no one sat.

As soon as I realized that I was in a hospital bed and that I had just awoken, I remembered how I had driven straight into a gigantic fir next to the road. I hadn't wanted to hit the big deer that had remained on the road, looking at me with that dumb expression, uninterested in moving and saving himself.

I had been in an accident then. A car accident.

Shane shot up from his chair, letting go of my hand. "I'll go tell grandma and grandpa. They'll be so happy you're finally awake."

Before I could say anything, he was out of the room. I turned to Beth, who seemed to have barely noticed Shane leaving she was so focused on me.

"How—how long have I been here?" I asked slowly, my mouth dry and my voice raspy.

"Almost three days. You were in a car accident. Your parents are down in the hospital cafeteria, having a meal. They left only minutes ago. We've all been here since you were taken here. Waiting for you to wake up after the operation. It took a lot longer than the doctors predicted. We were so worried we'd lost you."

I frowned and tried to lift my head to get a look at myself, my body. I discovered then that my entire left leg was in a cast and raised from the bed, hanging from a stand. Fear shot through me and I turned my attention back to Beth. "The operation? What happened? How bad was the accident? Am I going to be okay?"

Carefully, I watched her face as I asked the last question. I really wanted to know the truth now, and nothing but the truth. Even if it was bad. Better to hear about it now when we were alone.

"Yes, the doctors say you should be fine," Beth said and smiled warmly, sincerely, patting my arm. "You have a broken leg and a couple of broken ribs. Other than that, you're okay. As soon as your leg heals, you should be back to normal. As I said, we were just worried that it took you so long to wake up after the operation. It lasted twelve hours. But here you are." She squeezed my elbow and smiled encouragingly.

"What exactly did they operate on?"

"You had bone splints in your thigh that they had to remove. Lots of them apparently. You broke your femur. But everything went well putting it back together, and the doctors said you should be able to walk just fine again after some rehab."

"Oh." I nodded. "That's good, I guess."

The smile on Beth's lips shrank then and she turned serious. "What were you doing out driving so late anyway, Jennifer? I thought you told me you were home with Shane, who was really sick. But he wasn't. I found out as soon as he called me."

I looked at her, searching my brain for a reasonable explanation to her question. But things didn't move as efficiently up there as I was used to. Trying to use my head made it hurt. And before I could say anything at all, the door to my room opened. A balding, middle-aged man with a big nose and jowls stormed in. He was dressed in a white doctor's coat and held a chart in his hand. Behind him followed a small nurse with pin-straight, platinum hair.

"Ah, there you are at last," he said, beaming pleased. He came up to me and checked my vitals, using both hands and his stethoscope that hung around his thick neck. I noticed a brown suit and blue silk tie under the white coat. "I'm Dr. Cohen. We were beginning to worry you'd never come back you were sleeping so hard!" He winked at me to take the edge off his words. "How are you feeling, Jennifer?"

I tried to shrug, but I had a hard time moving my shoulders, I discovered. They were stiff and ached. "Not too bad, all things considered, I guess. I'm sorta thirsty."

"Here you go," the blond nurse said and handed me a paper mug filled with water. It was as if she'd expected me to ask for something to drink. I took it from her gratefully and chugged its contents.

"How does everything look?" I asked the doctor when I removed the cup from my lips.

"You sound and look good," he answered competently. "You were lucky you got away rather easily. I'm surprised you're not in worse shape, quite frankly. When you get a look at the front of your car, you'll know what I mean. It was a head-on collision. What made you drive off the road if I may ask? You had very little alcohol in your blood."

I gave a smirk. "There was a big stupid deer on the road all of a sudden. And he refused to move. I didn't want to hit him."

Dr. Cohen pinched his face and nodded understandingly. "I suppose that makes sense. Well, as I said, you got very lucky all the injuries you sustained were a broken femur and a couple of fractured ribs. The rest is minor, lots of bruises and scratches. You'll be back on your feet in no time."

"That's great to hear."

"You'll need some physical therapy once the leg's healed, but that's really it. And crutches for the next several weeks, of course. It'll make your upper body super strong!"

He kept reassuring me I'd be fine in that borderline inappropriate joking manner. I was glad he was the talkative kind who didn't really expect much in response. It allowed me to search my brain for what to tell Beth.

Unfortunately, it still didn't cooperate.

7

The doctor was done with me by the time Shane returned with my parents, having stayed for several minutes. I was to be discharged in a couple of days, when he could be certain my state was stable.

My mother, who'd always been prone to overly dramatic outbursts, nearly threw herself at me as she, Dad, and Shane entered the room. Shane was following closely behind, competing for space to get his arms around me. Dad hovered in the background. Before closing the door after herself, the nurse advised them to be careful, reminding them that I had a couple of broken ribs. Mom controlled herself before she could envelope me in a bear hug.

"Oh yes," she said, satisfying herself with merely rubbing my arm affectionately. "I almost forgot." She shot the nurse a warm smile. "Thank you, nurse."

Shane had stopped beside Mom and was holding my hand again, glancing at me with those golden-flecked teal eyes with the very long, dark eyelashes framing them. He had the most amazing eyes that he'd inherited from his father, alert and intelligent. He smiled at me, his dimples popping in his round face.

"How are you, Mom? I was so worried I'd never see you again."

Holding his gaze, I returned his smile at the same time as I tried to determine whether he had figured out I had lied to Beth yet. Had she told him when he called her? It was impossible to tell from his current expression, which bothered me. I struggled to come to grips with what was going on in my son's mind in general and right now, I could really use knowing. A disturbing image of him stabbing Macy entered my head instead and I instantly made it go away.

Well, he will tell me about it eventually, or tell Beth, I thought. Nothing to worry about, I silently reassured myself. I squeezed my son's large hand, which was almost the size of a man's while his body was not yet that big. While he had grown a lot lately, measuring five feet eight now, he was reedier than ever.

"I'm fine, honey, all things considered. How are you?"

"I'm good. When you didn't come home, I called Beth. She told me she had no idea where you were, but she thought it was only a matter of time before you got home and that I shouldn't worry."

I caught Beth's eye then, and I sensed that she was trying

to tell me something. It seemed she hadn't told him that I'd left her house hours earlier then. I focused on my son, who kept talking:

"But I *was* worried! I knew something bad had happened to you, Mom." His eyes filled with tears and he sniffled.

"You did?" I asked, a little thrown. It wasn't like Shane to act this emotional.

"Yes. I could *feel* it in my whole body. You know, like you say you can."

"Really? Did you tell Beth that?"

Shane turned his head and briefly glanced at Beth, who'd walked around to the end of the bed to give him and Mom space. Then he looked back at me again.

"No," he replied. "I didn't think of it until we hung up. It didn't hit me until then. I called your phone, but you didn't pick up."

"I was worried too," Beth inserted. "I really did think you'd be home any second, but when I didn't hear from Shane again, I called your phone to see what you were up to. I got voicemail as well, but it still took a while before I got real worried. That didn't happen until I called Shane thirty minutes later and asked if you were back and you weren't. So I drove over to your house to wait with him. It was four in the morning when we found out that you'd been in a car accident. A couple had passed you on the road and spotted you. They called for help. Thankfully, your purse was beside you on the passenger seat with your wallet and driver's license, so the authorities were able to identify you quickly. We got a call from them and were terrified."

"Your father and I nearly had a heart attack when we found out what had happened," Mom cut in, pressing a sun-spotted hand to her chest that was covered by a flower-patterned cotton dress. "We were sure you were dead. We came straight to the hospital in the morning when you were in the OR. As soon as we heard—which could've been sooner." She shot Beth a dirty look and harrumphed.

"Shane couldn't find your phone number," Beth explained sheepishly, avoiding my mother's stern gaze. I was grateful Mom let it go and merely shook her dyed head of strawberry-blond hair in response.

I nodded and asked, "How long was I out for?"

"A little over forty-eight hours," Shane replied. "The operation began at seven in the morning and it's nine now, so close to fifty."

You could always count on Shane to come up with such answers quickly. He had always excelled in every subject in school except for gym class. He had never been a particularly good athlete, mainly because he had no interest in sports. I had tried for the longest time to get him to take up a sport, but so far nothing had stuck. My next attempt involved soccer as he really needed to get off his butt more often. If only he had been as obsessed with sports as he was with taking pictures and drawing. Ever since he learned how to use a crayon, he'd been drawing or painting stuff. He also figured out how to use his father's camera the first time he was allowed to touch it. We quickly discovered that he was a born photographer with an eye for the right angle and color schemes. For his fifth birthday, he got his own camera to use. Plenty of his drawings and photos covered the walls in our house, and in our friends' houses as well.

"Thanks, honey," I said to Shane. I noticed that he was wearing a long-sleeved sweater and baggy shorts that ended right below his knobby kneecaps. There were some nasty scratches on his neck, and when I discreetly checked his hands, I noticed the same going on there. I felt my entire body relax. *He must have told me the truth then.*

"What did you do with Macy?" I asked him. "Is she—" Catching my parents and Beth with my peripheral vision, I cut myself off. How was I supposed to phrase what Shane had done to the cat? I didn't want to bring up the fact that he had essentially butchered Macy. Not without everyone knowing why first.

"What's wrong with Macy?" Mom asked, looking from me to Shane and then back again. She loves cats even more than I do.

"She's dead," Shane answered before I could say anything. "She had rabies, so I had to kill her. With a knife. It was either her or me," he added dramatically.

"She had rabies?" my dad blurted, finally saying something. He had always been a man of few words. "How the heck did the cat get rabies?"

"Probably from a bat or something," I explained. "This

part of the country is no longer rabies-free, Dad. That changed as of 2012. So about a year ago."

"Really?" Dad looked incredulous.

"Where's the cat now?" Mom asked.

Shane looked at her for a tense moment, then said, "She was so messy that I took her to the creek and threw her in the water."

8

I was alone with Shane an hour later. I had finally convinced my parents to go home and get some rest, and Beth had to go to work. Shane claimed that he wasn't tired at all, so I had allowed him to remain with me for a while longer. Normally, I would have sent him home with his grandparents, but I wanted to speak to him on my own.

"Can you remove the shirt for me?" I asked him a few minutes after my parents were gone.

"Why?" he protested, looking at me like I was nuts. "It's *cold* in here."

I gave him an encouraging smile. "You won't have to keep it off for long. I just want to see what Macy did to you. Please take it off, honey."

Grimacing, he pulled the large sweater over his head. I sucked in a breath and blocked my mouth when I saw the state of his skinny arms. They were covered with thin, long scratches, some of which were swollen and most of which were an angry red. I thought I could spot a few bite marks as well. There were a few scratches on his chest too, but not as serious-looking as the ones on his arms and neck.

"Oh my God, honey," I whispered, staring at the many scratches. "Macy really did a number on you, didn't she?"

He cocked a brow at me. "I told you, didn't I? Do you think I would've killed her otherwise? She was acting *crazy*. I seriously thought she had been possessed by a demon. Can I put on my shirt now?"

"Yes. Yes, of course. Put it on. Did you see a doctor yet?"

He scowled lightly. "No, why? I don't need to see a doctor. I just cleaned the scratches myself and put some anti-bacterial ointment on them and Band-Aids on some. They'll heal on their own. They already look a lot better. You should've seen me that night. *Phew.*" He wiped away imaginary sweat on his forehead with the back of his big hand. "If I'd have known you wouldn't be able to see them until now, I would've taken pics of the worst ones!"

I grabbed hold of his wrist and pulled him closer. "It's not a matter of the scratches, honey. You need *rabies shots*. Right away. You'll die if you caught the virus and it's allowed to develop. Don't you know that, you, who're so damned smart?" I nearly shrieked the last sentence, I was so terrified by the idea that Shane would die from having contracted rabies. It had suddenly dawned on me that rabies was deadly once you developed the disease. I had a vague memory of having read that you needed to get post-exposure shots immediately after being bitten by a rabies-infested animal or insect. How long was it since Shane had been bitten now? I narrowed my eyes and thought hard, ignoring the pain it produced in my head. It had to have been at least three days ago now. Was that too late? Oh God, don't let it be too late.

"You need to get those shots right now, Shane," I told him in a grave voice, tightening my grip around his wrist. "Get the doctor here. Tell him I need to speak to him. Go now and find the doctor for me, any doctor. Go, go." I let go of him, ushering him out of the room at the same time as I pressed the button for a nurse to come see me. I was desperate to see someone who could give Shane the shots and tell me it wasn't too late. Shane left the room and I kept pressing and pressing on the button.

It didn't take long for a nurse to enter the room. She was older than the other who'd been in the room earlier, gray-haired and with a lined face that had no makeup on it. She moved slowly, like she was in pain. Adjusting her wire-rimmed glasses, she peered at me.

"You called for assistance?"

"Yes. My son was bitten and scratched by a cat that had rabies a few days ago. He needs post-exposure rabies shots. How long does he have before it's too late for them to work?"

The nurse pursed her mouth. "I believe it's ten days, but I'm not entirely sure. I would have to double-check."

"Please go and do that now. For every second that passes,

my son could develop the disease. I can't have him die from rabies!"

She must have picked up on me turning frantic again, because she held up a hand and said, "I'll double-check for you. Please calm down. If it's only been a few days and he hasn't displayed any signs of the disease, he should be fine. I'll be right back."

She disappeared out of the room, leaving me alone with my panicked thoughts. It was getting increasingly hard for me to breathe. Had Shane shown any signs? What were the first signs anyway? I tried to remember what I had read in that article, but nothing of use came to me. I looked left and right in the room, at the table beside my bed, at the bench along the wall. Where was my phone? I needed my phone so I could google the answer. Damn it, where was my *phone?*

Another minute filled with agony passed until the door opened again and Shane came in with a doctor I didn't recognize.

"I couldn't find your doctor, so I brought Dr. Lunden," he explained.

Dr. Lunden, who was younger and more attractive than Dr. Cohen, gazed at me with an attentive face. "Your son has been bitten by a rabies-infected cat?"

"Yes, and he needs the shots right away. It happened three days ago. Or four. It's not too late, is it? Please tell me it's not too late."

"No, not at all." Dr. Lunden tossed a glance in Shane's direction. "How are you feeling, son?"

Shane shrugged his lanky shoulders. "Fine."

"Someone should also take a look at all the scratches and bite marks on his arms," I said. "Some of them are pretty bad."

The doctor nodded. "Sure thing. Why don't you come with me, Shane, and we'll have you looked over? We can do the shots here at the hospital."

A big smile stretched my lips and I relaxed. "Thank you so much, Dr. Lunden. I really, really appreciate it."

Telling me he was happy to help, the young doctor took my son with him out of the room.

9

I was back in the country house two days later, seated on the comfy blue couch in the living room, talking to Beth on the phone. My broken leg was resting on a side stool, while my other was curled up halfway under me. We hadn't gotten a chance to really talk until now, as it was the end of the month and Beth had been busy working on her company close-out. She was a sales rep for a health club and every last three days of the month, it was the same story—she was super busy trying to hit sky-high sales goals corporate had set for them. It was the best time to buy a gym membership as the sales reps gave people special deals, desperate to get their numbers up.

"You thought I had what?" I asked her. "An affair? How could I be having an affair when I'm a widow? Did you forget that? I can do whatever I want with whomever I want. There's no one to report to." Though I wish there were, I thought but didn't say, swallowing. I wasn't in the mood to go over yet again how much I missed Peter. No matter what Beth thought and I myself kept hoping, I very much doubted I would ever meet someone I loved as much as I had loved my dead husband. My throat tightened at an alarming rate and it got hard to breathe, so I quickly pushed further thoughts of him out of my mind.

"Okay, not an *affair*-affair, silly." She sighed theatrically. "I obviously know you can do whatever you want with whomever. I just thought it was a new thing that you wanted to keep secret for a while. You know, that it was the reason you didn't go straight home to Shane and why you lied to me. You did lie to me, you know."

"Yes, that's true. I did do that."

"So why did you lie to me? If you didn't meet up with your secret lover, where did you have to go? You obviously didn't have to go be with your son because he was so sick like you claimed. Though, I have to admit, he was quite pale and clammy when I got there. He also acted weird, like he was in shock or something. I thought it had to do with you missing and him being worried. He wasn't actually sick, was he?"

"No, no, he wasn't. He was in shock. Remember how Macy attacked him? He had no choice but to kill the cat. He felt terrible afterward. Very guilty. He really didn't want to have to kill the cat, but it was either him or the animal. You should see some of the marks on his arms. They're pretty bad."

She sucked in a breath. "Oh my God, I *totally* forgot about that. Poor thing. I do remember that he had some scratches on his hands now that I think about it. That was all I could see because he was wearing a hoodie with a big collar. Is he going to be okay?"

"Yes, he'll be fine. He got post-exposure rabies shots at the hospital, so it's all good now. None of the scratches are expected to leave scars, they told us."

"Good. So why did you lie to me?"

I searched my mind to come up with a plausible reason for my odd behavior. I still didn't feel like bringing Beth up-to-date regarding my son's psychopathic tendencies. It was better that I kept my son's secret from every single person, even my closest friends. Hell, I hadn't even told my mother with whom I was close. I didn't want *anyone* to know about Shane's state. All that would lead to would be them judging him, jumping to unfair conclusions. I didn't need that. My son didn't need that. Especially not since I would make sure he didn't do anything bad to anyone ever again. Thank God it had turned out he hadn't snapped in the end, stabbing the cat to death just because. Fixing him wouldn't be as hard as I had feared that night.

I considered how close I had been to telling Beth the truth when I had driven away from the country house, brutal images of Shane killing Macy firmly etched onto my retina. I had been dangerously close to spilling everything. But in the end something inside me had stopped me. I would have been furious with myself now, having realized it was just me freaking out, jumping to conclusions. As usual, there had been an acceptable explanation when all was said and done.

"Hello, Jen? Are you still there?"

My brain was unable to produce a suitable alternative to Beth's accusation, so I did the second best—I went with hers. It wasn't bad actually.

"Yeah, sorry," I said and let out a defeated breath. "Okay, I confess: I *did* go meet up with a guy. I met him at the post office in town the other day. I didn't want you to know about it, or anyone else. Not after all the disappointments I've been through since I started dating again. This time I *promised* myself that I wouldn't tell anyone about my latest guy before I'd gone out with him a few times and it had developed into something. I've realized something about myself—the only reason I get upset about guys I barely know rejecting me is because everyone's asking me for the latest status. And I can't blame them for asking me when I keep talking nonstop about the latest guy I'm excited about! Honestly, when all's said and done, I haven't been all that excited about anyone really. I only thought I was at the time. But a few weeks later, I can't even remember their names." In reality, no one ever measured up to Peter in the end, but I wasn't about to admit that out loud. It wouldn't help me move on.

Beth chuckled. "Ha! I guess you're right about that. It's smarter to let things develop a bit before you start obsessing about them."

"Exactly," I said a little too quickly and with a little too much emphasis.

"So it was another loser then?"

"What was?"

"The guy you went to see when you lied to me, silly! What *else* could I be talking about?"

"Oh right, sorry. The painkillers I'm on are making it hard for my brain to function properly."

"I thought you told me you hadn't taken any painkillers 'cause you didn't have any pain."

Damn it. "I said that? Well, there you go. Those friggin' pills are making me forget *everything.*" I cleared my throat and rambled on. "Yeah, Dan was a real loser. I honestly wasn't sure what had attracted me to him in the first place. I should never have given him my phone number. It took me until the main entrée to conclude that, though, so that's why I stayed so long. I suppose I wanted to give the guy a chance. He was trying so damned hard. I felt sorry for him."

"What was wrong with him?"

"Well, first of all, he was totally obsessed with himself. All he did was talk about what he did and where he was from. But what was even worse was this annoying thing he did with his tongue."

"What did he do with his tongue?"

"It kept shooting out of his mouth like a reptile's, swiping his lower lip like a windshield wiper. I swear, I think he has some kind of condition and forgot to take his meds or something. Cause he sure didn't do that weird thing when we spoke at the post office or I'd never have gone out with him."

"Oh wow. Poor guy. Maybe he was nervous."

"Yeah, that's what I thought too at first, which was why I decided to stay till dessert. You know, to give him a chance. But I don't think it was nerves. The guy's what, forty? He can't be *that* nervous on a first date any longer. Anyway, that tongue tic turned me off even more than his self-absorption, so when we were done eating, I told him I had to call it a night. My son was at home waiting for me."

"How much wine did you have?"

"Only a glass and a half. I wasn't even tipsy. I really don't think I drove off that road because I was intoxicated. By the time I was driving home, at least an hour had passed since I had the last wine."

"They didn't check your alcohol levels, did they?"

"Yes, they did. And the doctor said my alcohol levels were low."

"Oh, okay."

We spoke some more, finishing the conversation by settling on a time for Beth to come over and have dinner with me and Shane the following night.

When I had disconnected the call, I placed the phone to my chest. I pricked up my ears to check if I could hear the sound of Shane playing video games in his bedroom. Playing video games was one of his favorite pastimes, second to editing photos on his computer. After dinner tonight, he'd gone straight to his room to play his latest obsession, *Killing the Hare.* That's when I went to the living room to enjoy a glass of red while catching up with Beth.

The faintest sound of firing guns reached my ears. *Good,* I thought. I preferred that he stayed in his room tonight. I needed time alone. Time to pore over what had happened in the last week.

Shane had gotten his rabies shots at the hospital and was fine, just like Dr. Lunden had promised. He'd also had his scratches and bite marks attended to. They were healing quickly.

It did disturb me that he had tossed Macy's body in the creek. I suppose I could see why he had chosen to do it, but I had really wanted to have the cat checked for rabies. If I knew the cat had rabies, I could be one hundred percent sure Shane had told me the truth. As it was, I had this niggling feeling inside me that he had just made it up, feigned all the scratches and bite marks on his arms. Well, there were mostly scratches. It would be hard to do, but it was unfortunately possible nonetheless. As I had taken a closer look at them, I had reluctantly concluded that.

I swallowed the rest of the wine and shook my head. I really needed to stop thinking about this. *Of course* he had told me the truth.

10

Four weeks later, I had succeeded in putting the disturbing incident with Shane and Macy behind me. All the scratches and bruises from my accident were gone. I was mastering moving around the house with my crutches and my broken ribs were almost fully healed. My thigh bone was doing well, too. According to my doctor and the physical therapist I was working with, if I kept up the good work, I would be able to ditch the crutches in a month and a half. I could hardly wait. I might be a lot better at using them now that I'd developed more upper body strength, but that didn't mean I liked being forced to use them. It was still a pain to get around with them, especially outside, like when I had to take the subway, for example. I'd come to learn the hard way that people in Queens where we lived weren't any friendlier or more helpful than busy Manhattanites. Sadly, I couldn't drive a car in my condition, so I had to rely on public transportation. I wasn't about to waste money on cab rides when one could take the bus or the subway everywhere. We weren't that rich and frankly, at least the subway was typically much faster than driving. Fortunately, I didn't have to use either very often.

After having spent most of August followed by Labor Day weekend upstate, Shane and I were back to our regular lives. That meant he was in school, in seventh grade to be exact, and I was working from home as well as keeping up with the latest research relating to psychopathy. Thankfully, being a developmental editor for an online romance publisher named Lovestruck, I had the kind of job that didn't require me to go into the office. I went through manuscripts at home. In fact, my boss encouraged me to use my study as my main office, as the company in Brooklyn was tiny and usually crowded. The company had several employees, but little space for us to work. The only times I really needed to be there were when we had staff meetings that couldn't take place over Skype.

I had been working for Lovestruck for almost two years now and I enjoyed it, as it involved using my creative side. I had begun as an editorial assistant and quickly worked myself up to taking on my own manuscripts. The pay wasn't amazing, but it did pay our bills, of which there were plenty, not to mention part of the rent. Shane and I were still making do on the money Peter had left us, but the account was thinning out. Lovestruck was doing well, though, so I expected to get a substantial wage increase soon. One way or another we would be okay.

I missed not writing on a screenplay, but I couldn't imagine doing it again, even if I had the time to mess around at home. Not when it had—indirectly—resulted in my husband's death. The mere thought of starting another screenplay made me physically ill. Editing other people's stories allowed me to at least live out their characters in my head.

Peter had been anything but creative, so Shane must have gotten his genes from me. He really was a talented artist and even more talented photographer. The very best of his paintings and pictures hung on the living room walls in our apartment, some of them framed. When people visited us, they often commented on how stunning they were, how different and creative. How Shane was born to become an artist. As he had gotten older, he focused more and more on photography and editing as opposed to drawing and painting. These days he took pics using his smartphone, as the camera in it was almost as good as his regular one and it was always with him. In the evenings, he often showed me amazing shots he'd taken during the day. He kept improving.

This morning Shane had overslept and forgotten to bring his phone when he took off for school. I couldn't remember the last time that had happened. He kept that phone next to him every second of the day, even when he went into the bathroom to take a shower. It was like it was a part of him and he couldn't function without it.

I found his phone on top of a chest of drawers in his bedroom when I went there to see if he had any sour patch candy lying around somewhere. It was my favorite kind of sweets. I usually had a big bag of it a few times a week, but now that I couldn't move as much as I should, I needed to be careful that I didn't gain weight. I stopped buying it whenever I went to the grocery store. Yesterday I had caught Shane eating some in his room that he must have picked up on his way home from school. Unlike me, he didn't eat the whole bag, so I was hoping I could score the remaining pieces. A few wouldn't make much difference in my waistline, I told myself.

But the only thing of interest that I spotted when I entered his room was his forgotten phone. There was no candy anywhere in sight, unfortunately.

Oh well, I thought and grabbed the phone. It was for the best. The sudden candy urge would go away soon anyway. If it didn't, I'd have an apple instead. Much healthier. With the phone in the pocket of my sweatpants, I made my way out of his room and back to my home office. I'd work another couple of hours and then I'd go make myself some lunch.

As I was about to go into the kitchen and prepare something to eat, my own cell phone rang. I sat back down in the chair and picked it up from the desk. I didn't recognize the number on the screen. Pressing Talk, I placed the phone to my ear.

"Hello."

"Mom? It's me, Shane."

"Hi, honey. Everything okay?"

"Yeah. I forgot my phone, so I'm calling from Leo's phone. I need something I saved on my phone for school, though. Can you get it for me? It should be in my room."

"It's already in my pocket. I went into your room earlier to see if you had any candy left for me. I saw your phone on the drawers, so I took it with me."

"Oh. Sorry, there's no more candy. I ate it all yesterday. Can you pull up a thing for me and email it to me? I saved it in the Notes app."

"Of course. Hold on while I get it out."

I stuck my hand into the pants pocket and pulled up his phone. "Okay, I'm ready. What's your password?"

He gave it to me.

I punched in the numbers and the screen opened. "I'm in. What should I be looking for again?"

"Go to the Notes app and find the paragraph I wrote about China. It's called 'China'. Then email it to me. You should be able to email it to me directly from the app."

"Okay, hang on." I put my own phone down and got to work. I wasn't a technical whizz and Shane had an iPhone while I had a Samsung one, but I still managed to not only find what he'd wanted, but also to email it to him. I grabbed my phone when I was done.

"Okay, done," I told him. "Check your email and see if you got it."

"I'm checking right now." A moment of silence ensued, then, "Okay, I got it. Thanks, Mom. Want me to buy you some sour patches on my way home from school?"

I laughed. "No, honey, I'm good. I really need to watch my

weight."

"Okay. See you later."

I disconnected the call and put my own phone down next to Shane's. I wasn't sure what compelled me to pick up his again and go through it; all I know was that, a minute later, I had forgotten all about making myself lunch and was deeply immersed in my son's cellular life. In particular, I was fascinated by all the amazing pics he'd taken using his phone. He really was an incredible photographer. Many of them were of things up in the Catskills, like of a tree or a rock with moss growing on it. Landscapes in the woods. A few were of the old buildings and the lake there. Each seemed better, more interesting than the last. I was already mentally picking out which ones we could blow up and frame. My parents would love to have some of them in their house.

It was when I got to the pics of Alice that I nearly dropped the phone.

At first, I wasn't sure what I was looking at, as the first pics were close-ups of her body. It took me a few and when I did, I gasped out loud.

I stared at a shot of Alice lying on the ground, spread-eagled. There was an unevenly edged blood halo around her head and shoulders on the light gray stone underneath her. The long, blond ponytail stuck out from under her head, part of it smeared with the dark red blood. There were a couple of close-ups of the bloodied ponytail, of her face. Her clear blue eyes stared heavenward, fear and confusion imprinted in them.

As if possessed, I kept swiping the screen and discovered more disturbing pics of Alice lying face-up on the stony ground, taken from different angles. Each photo seemed more brutal than the next.

I felt faint as I paged through the pics of the dead girl, maybe fifteen in total. When I'd reached the last, I went back to the beginning, going through all of them again as if that would make them less conspicuous. What were these pics doing in my son's phone? I couldn't think of another explanation than him having taken them himself. That meant he must have been present the day Alice had fallen from the cliff in the woods, fallen to her death, shattering her skull.

Why hadn't he told me that he'd been there? We would have found Alice much sooner had he told me and everyone else. The authorities estimated that she had been dead for at least 24 hours by the time she'd been found by the search teams.

What had Shane been doing out in the woods with Alice? He had told me he'd spent the day with the neighbor's kids where they had played a card game.

So he had lied to me then? He must have. He never lied to me. I put down his phone next to my computer and rested my head in my hand, closing my eyes and inhaling deeply through my nostrils. Nausea was building inside me. Oh God. Oh God. This was so not what I'd needed to see. But I had. The pics were for real.

What the hell should I do?

11

I had yet to get a hold of Jacob Gardner when Shane got home from school a few hours later. I had called his parents, Lisa and Eric, twice since I'd discovered those disturbing pics in my son's phone. Lisa hadn't been around, so I left her a voicemail, telling her I really needed to speak to her and Jacob as well as to his older sister Zelda as soon as possible. Eric had picked up, but he had been late for a meeting and had not had time to talk to me; he promised to call back when he got home, though.

Never before had time passed as slowly as it did that day, every minute feeling like an hour. I was dying to pace the apartment, but it was too difficult with the crutches; I had to make do shifting around in my chair instead. That didn't relieve all the nervous energy inside me, but it was better than nothing.

I needed to know if Shane had been with Jacob and

Zelda the day of Alice's death, and if they had been at home all day.

It had dawned on me that someone might have forwarded the pics to my son's phone. I couldn't tell if he himself had taken the pics; trust me, I'd already checked. Why someone would forward such pics was a mystery, of course, not to mention still extremely weird, but I liked that explanation better than Shane himself being the photographer.

When the front door opened in the hallway and Shane called out, "Hi, Mom! I'm home," I was a nervous wreck. My nails were chewed down to the quick. No matter how I twisted and turned this situation around in my head, I couldn't come up with a reason for Shane having all those pics in his phone that didn't upset me. Even him just having spotted her and decided to take pics was a major problem. I mean, who *did* that? Wouldn't he at least tell me about having seen her when he was back home? But he hadn't. There was no explanation for that.

As I heard him approach the study, I no longer thought someone having forwarded him the pics was a real possibility. That was just wishful thinking. It really didn't look like that at all. He, or someone using his phone, had taken them. The pics fell well within the timeframe the medical examiner had estimated Alice's time of death to be, yet her body hadn't been discovered until the following afternoon. Shane had clearly known she was dead. Why hadn't he told anyone about it? Why had a search team been forced to find her, wasting hours, when Shane had known where she'd been all along?

My son stuck his head into my home office where I sat behind the computer, trying to edit a manuscript. Ever since I'd spotted those photos, I had been useless, though. I kept reading and rereading the same page, the words and letters flowing together, becoming indecipherable. But I didn't know what else to do but to keep trying to make sense of it, so I'd kept going.

"Hi, what are you doing?" he asked, peering at me, his light brown hair messy.

I managed a weak smile. "I'm trying to work. Editing this historical romance. It's not going so well."

He kept looking at me, narrowing his eyes. "Are you okay?"

I ran a hand through my long, blond hair in an attempt to shield my face; I worried the anxiety I was filled with showed. "Yeah, I'm just a little tired. I may be coming down with something. How was school?"

Shane rolled his eyes. "Boring as usual. I'm already done with this semester's math and science classes."

"That's great, honey! Are you hungry?"

"Yeah, a little."

I pushed myself out of my chair and grabbed my crutches. "Okay, let's go make something to eat then. What are you in the mood for?"

"Pizza."

I chuckled stiffly. "Why did I even have to ask? Well, we

won't be having pizza right now. We've been eating far too much pizza lately. What about some pasta with meat sauce and a salad? That's almost as good as pizza, isn't it? I think so. Yes, it's definitely better than pizza."

Stop rambling, Jennifer, I silently ordered myself. I inhaled deeply through my nose in an attempt to settle down. *You'll only make things worse for both of you if he realizes how upset you are. Surely, there will turn out to be a perfectly understandable explanation as to why those pics are in Shane's phone. Just like there had been one to explain the cat incident. Something you haven't even thought of.*

"Not really," Shane commented and made a grimace. "But it's fine. Where's my phone?"

"Right there." I nodded with my head at the shiny device next to my laptop. Shane reached his arm out and snatched it up, scrolling through it.

Fear shot through me when he paused and a deep furrow formed between his eyebrows.

Had he noticed that I had been in his phone and seen the pics of dead Alice?

What would he do if he did?

As suddenly as he had paused and scowled, his face relaxed and he let out a loud guffaw.

"Mom, you've got to see this," he said and held the phone before my eyes. A video from Facebook was displayed on the screen. It showed a kitten and a huge dog fighting each other, the kitten clearly dominating the dog. "It's so funny!"

I had to admit that it was pretty funny, so I, too, found myself laughing despite my dark mood. Which helped me relax a little.

He turned around and walked out to the kitchen. I ambled after him on my crutches as best I could. I had nearly entered the kitchen when my phone rang. It was in my pocket.

Shane grabbed the phone out of my pants before I could stop him. He checked the screen and then answered.

"Hi, Mrs. Gardner, how are you?" he said, looking at me with a big grin. He knew I really didn't like it when he answered my phone for me. Today it bothered me more than ever when I heard who was calling.

"Give me the phone right away, Shane," I ordered him. But he didn't; instead, he stepped away so I couldn't reach him, making me furious.

"No, I don't know what was so important, but you can ask her yourself," he said into the phone. "She's right here. Hang on."

Finally, he handed me the phone and I snatched it from him with a huff, my heart pounding faster. As I leaned against a counter and placed the phone to my ear, I glared at him. He answered by giggling delightfully. He could be such a pain.

"Hi, Lisa," I said into the phone. "Thanks for calling me back."

"It sounded very important. Is everything okay?"

"Oh yes, there was just something I wanted to discuss with you." My eye caught Shane then. He had stopped giggling and was staring at me instead, his face watchful. Overly curious. Now was not the time to talk to Lisa about where my son had been the day Alice had died. "But Shane and I were just about to eat something. Would it be okay if I called you back later?"

"Sure. I should be around the rest of the evening. Just give me a shout when you get the chance."

"Great, thanks. Bye."

I extended the phone to Shane. "Can you please put that on the kitchen table for me? My charger is on the floor. I need to charge my phone. And stop answering my calls. You know that it really annoys me."

He looked surprisingly sheepish as he squatted to pick up the charger cord. "Sorry. It's just so much fun when you get annoyed."

I glared at him. "Keep that up and you'll see me get real annoyed. I don't think you'll like that as much."

He didn't answer and just stuck the charger into my phone. I walked up to the stove to get the frying pan out from where I kept it in the oven. Doing so was a chore given the crutches, which was why we had ordered pizza more than usual recently. The crutches were really getting on my nerves, but we needed to eat some regular food now.

Shane hurried up to me and helped me get the pan out and onto the right cooking plate.

"Thanks," I muttered. "Now please get me the meat sauce from the freezer. It should be in the second drawer. In one of the blue plastic containers."

While he got that, I switched on the plate and poured a few drops of olive oil into the pan. Without a word, he handed me the container with the frozen meat sauce. I filled a pot with water for the pasta and put it on another plate, adding salt.

"Please set the table now," I said. "It won't take long before the food's ready."

He did as I wanted while I waited for the frying pan to heat up sufficiently. A minute later, it had and I poured the container's contents into the pan. Using a wooden fork, I mixed it around, trying to chop it up with the fork so that it thawed sooner.

"Are you okay, Mom?" Shane suddenly asked. He had set the table and also gotten the lettuce, tomatoes, and cucumbers out for the salad. I turned to him and he gazed at me with a face so filled with worry I felt a pang of guilt in my chest. Maybe I had been too harsh with him, snapping like that. He was just a twelve-year-old boy, full of energy. So he liked to be mischievous and pull pranks on me. It wasn't the end of the world.

I smiled at him. I wanted to ruffle his hair, but I couldn't or I'd risk falling to the floor. My other hand was busy thawing the meat sauce. "Yes. Like I said earlier, I'm just not feeling great today. I'm sorry that I snapped at you earlier."

"It's okay. I know I'm a handful." He grinned big at me, and I couldn't help returning it.

I sighed. "Yes, God knows you aren't always easy to deal with."

12

I made sure that Shane was busy editing photos on his computer when I returned Lisa's phone call a few hours later.

"Hi, Jennifer," Lisa said by way of answering.

"Hi, Lisa. Thanks for calling me back earlier. Are you busy?"

"Not at all. I was just watching a boring movie. I can use a break from it. What's up?"

"Do you remember the day when Alice Tate was found dead in the woods upstate back in May? Or, rather, the day before?"

"Oh, yeah. It's hard to forget. That was such an awful day. I feel so bad for Chris and Lana. I don't know what I would do if one of my kids fell off a cliff and died. I don't think I would ever get over it."

No, you wouldn't. It's almost as bad as your only child

shooting your husband to death, I thought. You definitely don't get over stuff like that. You pretend you do, but you don't. We had only known Lisa and her family since they bought their upstate country house near ours a couple of years ago. As far as I knew, neither she nor her husband was aware of what Shane and I had been through, and that was a good thing. So all I said was, "I know, it's awful what happened. Truly incomprehensible. So you remember that day then?"

"Yes, of course. How could I forget? Why do you ask?"

I had thought long and hard what reason I would give Lisa here. I couldn't just come out and tell her straight out that I feared my son might be connected to Alice's death. Worse, that he might be the one who'd pushed her. At last I came up with something I considered decent enough to tell her, which was this: "Shane spent the day playing cards with Jacob the day before Alice was found. He says that he brought a copy of *The Count of Monte Christo* for Zelda to read when he went over to your house. I've been looking for that book. Do you know if Zelda still has it?"

"I have absolutely no idea. Do you want me to ask her? I can do that right now. She's sitting right here beside me."

"Yeah, sure. That would be great."

I already knew what the answer would be—Zelda couldn't remember Shane having brought over such a book to lend her that day. Squeezing my cheek to my neck to keep the phone in place, I massaged cream into my hands while I waited for Lisa to get back to me. They tended to get dry all the time lately.

"Hey," she said about fifteen seconds later. "Zelda said he didn't bring over any book for her that day. Are you sure it was that day?"

"Yes, because Shane told me it was the day before they found Alice in the woods that he brought it over. He spent the day playing cards with Jacob and Zelda then."

"Hang on," Lisa said and there was some rustling as she moved the phone. "Are you *sure* Shane didn't bring you a book that day, Zelda?"

I could hear Zelda talking animatedly in the background, but not what she was saying.

"He did?" Lisa asked.

I assumed she'd meant the question for Zelda, not me. Zelda said something else that I couldn't make out.

"Jen?"

"Yeah?"

"She told me she's absolutely sure, and that I can ask Jacob for verification. It sounds like Jacob and Shane got into a fight over something with the card game; apparently, Shane stormed out of the house a few minutes later. I remember that part myself now that I think about it. I had just finished baking an apple pie and asked Shane if he wanted some. He told me he wasn't hungry and that he was going home. Then he strode to the front door and got out without saying goodbye. It was a bit rude, actually."

A chill went through me. All I could think of was that Shane had not been with Jacob and Zelda that entire day like he'd claimed. "You're saying that Shane left your house?"

"Yes."

"Do you remember what time? Approximately?"

"Hmm. I think it was around noon. Yes, it was right before noon because that's when I take that yoga class at the club in town. I remember thinking that I wouldn't have time to go that day. I had totally misjudged how long it would take me to bake the pie."

"Did Shane come back later?"

"No, I don't think so. Let me ask Zelda to be sure. Hold on. Zelda, did Shane come back to play cards with you guys again that day?"

Zelda responded something unintelligible.

"Zelda says she and Jacob didn't talk to him until the next day, when we all went in the search party for poor Alice."

So he had definitely lied to me then. Oh God. This was so not good. Oh God.

"Jen? Are you still there?"

"Oh, I'm such an idiot," I exclaimed, realizing that I had been silent for too long. "I mixed up the days."

"What do you mean?" Lisa sounded confused.

I made myself chuckle lightly. "You're right, Shane was home with me that day. And now that I think about it, I don't think he meant your Zelda."

"My Zelda?"

"Yes. I think he was referring to a Zelda in his class. I'm sorry. I'm completely out on a limb. Forget I even called. I need to call someone else to get that book back. Your Zelda doesn't have it. I'm sorry for wasting your time."

"No worries."

We exchanged a few more words, then I said goodbye, feeling lightheaded, nervous. This was so not the way I had hoped this conversation would go. A tiny part of me had clung to the possibility that Shane had been with Jacob and Zelda all day, and that someone had taken his phone and used it to take pics of dead Alice. The real killer, someone who wanted to set up my son. Someone who knew that he was the perfect target given his genetics. Someone who had found out that he had shot his father when he was only six.

The idea had popped into my head at some point and had lingered there only to crash and burn now. Shane had not been with Jacob and Zelda, nor had he gone home like he'd told Lisa. I, too, remembered clearly what I had been doing the day before Alice was found. I had been working on a romantic comedy novel and needed to be done that same night. When Shane told me he was going over to Jacob and Zelda's to play a card tournament, I remember clearly how pleased I had been. I got a lot more done when Shane wasn't around. He had a tendency to ask me a million and one questions throughout the day, and I didn't have the heart to tell him to leave me alone so I could work.

I tried to remember what time Alice had been estimated dead. Had it been before noon or after? But I couldn't, primarily because I'd had no reason to know about it, and it wasn't like Lana and Chris had announced the time of death, either. Why would they? The death had been deemed an accident. A freak accident, but still an accident. Fourteen-year-old Alice Tate had been an enthusiastic bird-watcher, and May was a great time to spot lots of species. The day before she was found dead, her neck broken and her skull shattered, she had told her parents that she would go out scouting for birds, as it had been a beautiful, clear day. She had brought her binoculars and sandwiches to eat and water to drink in a small backpack. It would be an all-day excursion.

It wasn't until the next day that everyone in the area realized that Alice had not returned home from her bird-watching excursion. Lana and Chris and Beth went knocking on everyone's door at nine in the morning to see if maybe Alice had spent the night there. Why she would ever do such a thing without telling her parents I still can't figure out, but I guess when you're panicking as much as the Tate's had done that morning, you didn't think things through. It didn't take long until the authorities had been alerted to Alice missing, and a search party was established that combed through the woods where Alice was thought to have gone. The trees, primarily fir, pine trees, and oaks, grew plentiful and tall there, and for miles without any people around.

Alice had been found beneath a small mountain on which a few large trees grew. The detective investigating the death had determined that she had climbed one of those trees, likely in search of a bird's nest or an even better view of the birds in that area. There had been broken branches in the pine tree right above where she had been found on a large stone shelf thirty yards below. The death had been instantaneous from what I had been able to understand.

That I still believed. Unfortunately, I also believed my son had been the one taking all those upsetting photos of Alice. The question now was what to do about it.

13

I went to bed that night without confronting Shane. When reality had sunk all the way in, I decided that I definitely needed to talk to him about the photos, see what he had to say about them. For a few crazed seconds, I had actually pondered pretending I had no idea about them. Sticking my head in the sand was obviously not an option. But it was too soon; I needed more time to process what I had discovered. More time to figure out the best way to broach the subject. I'd sleep on it and see how I felt about it the next morning. The fact of the matter was that, even if Shane had been involved in Alice's death, me confronting him about it wouldn't bring her back to life. In other words, there was no rush. Really, it would only serve to bring me clarity to a problem I secretly resented was mine to deal with. I preferred to wallow in denial for as long as possible.

I slept fitfully that night, waking up about once an hour despite having taken extra pills. By the time it was seven in the morning and the sky had brightened outside my bedroom window, I gave up trying to get more rest. It was time to deal with my life. My tossing and turning hadn't been all bad, though, as it had produced one useful result: Instead of confronting Shane right away, I had decided that I would go see my old therapist, talk to him about how to best deal with the situation. I simply couldn't stomach the idea of asking Shane straight out about the pictures in his phone. I needed guidance in how to do that. Consulting with a mental health professional before broaching something this delicate was likely the wisest approach. Surely, Dr. Wilkins would give me valuable advice how to talk to Shane about the pics. It wasn't exactly something you discussed every day.

As soon as Shane had gone to school that morning, I found Dr. Wilkins's contact information in my phone. I had seen him for a few months after Peter's death, then I'd felt there was nothing left for us to discuss. I felt better, like I could go on with life and cope with reality on my own, be a good mother to my son. So I'd stopped going.

I had never revealed to Dr. Wilkins that my son had been born with psychopathic tendencies. I hadn't dared doing so at the time. I knew that Dr. Wilkins had a professional obligation to keep quiet about Shane's condition, but I still didn't want to tell him. No one, absolutely no one, could know about it. It was too risky. What if it accidentally slipped out of Dr. Wilkins's mouth when he was drunk at a cocktail party or at dinner with a hot date? Maybe he wanted to show off his vast knowledge about a kid who'd accidentally shot his father, whose mother he was treating? Reveal secrets that had been kept from the public, such as the kid might develop into a full-fledged psychopath due to his flawed brain? If only there was a way to determine that people with such brains always became dangerous psychopaths, then we could have them institutionalized before they could inflict harm on others. Save all the innocent people. Exactly like in the movie *Minority Report*...

The chance that Dr. Wilkins would ever do something like that was unlikely, but still a possibility. So I'd kept the secret. Besides, my plan had been to make sure Shane didn't hurt anyone else again, so what was the point telling anyone about it? I'd watch him like a hawk. Everyone would be fine. Everything would be fine.

Too bad it seemed I hadn't watched him as closely as I had promised myself.

I had gotten lax in my supervision, mostly because Shane had been such a great kid after we had dealt with Peter's death. As the years passed and he continued to behave exemplary, there were times I forgot he was born a psychopath. I could no longer be sure to keep the promise I had made to myself. Well, it looked like I might have already broken it. While I'd of course try my best to ensure Shane didn't hurt yet another person, I couldn't be with him 24/7. Besides, if he had indeed killed Alice, he needed to pay for it. Make amends. I couldn't just let him get away with it. What kind of precedent would *that* set? I hoped it wouldn't be that bad, of course, and that he had only shown bad judgment in taking the pics and then stayed silent about it. It would be understandable, as, having taken them, people might think he was also behind her death. I had to take the right precautions, see to it that I did the right thing here and that everyone was safe, including my son. I had to talk to someone about it, and my old therapist seemed to be the safest person to do that with. Dr. Wilkins was not allowed to report a crime that had already been committed, so I risked nothing. If I didn't tell him I knew for a fact Shane was a psychopath who'd experienced trauma in his formative years, he'd also have no reason to go to the authorities and warn them about what my son might do in the future.

Shane would be safe while Dr. Wilkins advised me on how to deal with him.

I left a message on the therapist's voicemail and told him that I needed to see him again.

He called me back an hour later.

"Hi there, Jennifer," he said in that incredibly soothing voice of his. "It's been a while. Everything okay with you? You sounded tense in the message you left me. More than I can remember you've ever sounded."

I couldn't believe how good his memory was. It was at least five years ago since I'd spoken with him last. With all the patients he saw, how could he know who I was so quickly? But I guess that was a good thing.

"Yeah, I know," I said and let out an awkward chuckle. Unfortunately, the fact that he remembered me so easily must also mean he remembered how rudely I'd ended our therapy. "Sorry about just disappearing like that. I really did think I was coming back after the break I took."

"Oh, no worries. I wasn't offended at all. So, what's going on with you? Something's happened?"

"Well, I guess you could say that. I need to see you. I could use some advice on how to cope with some stuff. Do you have any openings in your schedule?"

"Let's see... Could you come tomorrow at one o'clock? Or do you need to see me today? I might have a slot later."

"No, tomorrow's fine. One works great. Thanks so much. See you tomorrow then."

The day moved at a snail's pace followed by another night of poor sleep. I arrived at Dr. Wilkins's office at a quarter to one and spent the remainder of the time flipping through old health and fitness magazines in the small waiting space.

The door to his office opened at a minute to one and a gray-haired woman dressed in black with red-rimmed eyes exited, avoiding my gaze. When she had left the area and I was alone, the door opened again and Dr. Wilkins appeared in the doorway. An average-looking man in his fifties, he glanced at me with a compassionate expression. His round face was as always clean-shaven and a pair of horn-rimmed glasses sat on the prominent nose, magnifying somewhat his beady eyes. He had a high forehead made even higher because of his semi baldness. What hair he had left was a mousy brown-gray color and grew in a fringe around his head like a monk's. Instead of a suit, he wore a dreary-colored cardigan over a button-down dress shirt and dark slacks that looked comfortable. His clothes were on the bigger side but still failed to camouflage his potbelly.

He smiled, revealing teeth that were uneven and could use some bleach, and motioned for me to enter his office. He did a double take when he realized I was on crutches. My leg was still wrapped up, but I wore loose linen pants that effectively hid this fact.

He stared at me as I made my way toward him.

"Oh dear. Whatever happened to you?" he asked, holding the door for me so I could enter.

"I was in a little car accident a while ago. I just need a few more weeks on these crutches and then I'll be back to normal. Well, kind of. I'll probably need a cane for a while."

"Hmm. Can't have been *that* little," he commented in a soothing voice and closed the door behind me. "Well, it's good to see you, Jennifer." He went around the small desk while I took a seat on the dark green wingchair he used for his patients. Still the same chair after all these years, I couldn't help but note. I hoped he had it cleaned once in a while. I crossed my legs and leaned back into the well-worn seat. He intertwined his sausage-like fingers before him and peered at me through his glasses.

"Tell me, what's going on with you, my friend?" he asked casually.

"It's my son. I found these very upsetting pics in his phone and I don't know what to do about it." I had pondered pretending this was some other kid, a friend's son, but at the last second, I'd changed my mind. Not only would it be hard for me to keep track of all the lying, but Dr. Wilkins would see through me sooner or later, and then I would have wasted all this time. I would just have to do my best so he didn't realize what I really feared was my son posing a threat to society in general.

"About the pictures in his phone?"

"Yes. The other day I accidentally spotted pictures taken of a dead girl. About fifteen of them."

"Go on."

"It was of a girl who'd fallen to her death from a mountain upstate. Well, a tree on a mountain. She slipped from one of the branches."

"Is this a girl your son knew?"

"Yes. We all knew her. She was the daughter of people who live near my parents' country house in the Catskills. Friends of mine actually. My son and I go there on the weekends and during the summer." I shifted in the chair.

Dr. Wilkins nodded pensively. "And you found pictures of the girl in your son's phone? You mean after she had fallen to her death?"

"Uh-huh."

"Have you asked him why they are there?"

I smiled awkwardly. "No. For some reason I can't make myself do it. That's why I called you."

"I see. Why do you think you can't make yourself ask him?"

I turned my head and glanced out the one window in the man's office. It showed a quiet road and some trees with red and yellow leaves against a gray, clouded backdrop. A green sedan drove by.

"Jennifer? Why can't you make yourself ask your son about the photos?"

Finally, I turned my head so I was facing Dr. Wilkins again. I sighed heavily. "I'm dead scared he has something to do with her death."

14

"Do you think he killed her?" Dr. Wilkins asked, removing his glasses and rubbing the root of his nose.

I stared at him, a little shocked by the bluntness of his question. It wasn't like him to be so direct. But that's what I had come for, wasn't it? I needed to have those words spelled out for me by someone else. I was too much of a coward to deal with them on my own.

"That is my fear, yes," I replied slowly. There, finally I'd said it. I reached for the small wooden hourglass that he always brought with him from home and put on the desk, careful not to turn it over in case he was using it to time our session. I supposed he was worried that the other two therapists who also used this office might steal it from him. The slightly pink sand inside it, which seemed full of tiny jewels it glittered so much, was making its way into the bottom part. I don't know why I had suddenly grabbed it, but something about it was soothing. Holding it in my hands and watching the sand pile up made me feel better. I tossed Dr. Wilkins a glance to see if my action bothered him. He didn't appear to mind, his attention on my face, not the hourglass.

"Do you think it might have been an accident?" he asked.

"I don't know. That would of course be preferable over it having been done intentionally. But I don't understand why he would take photos of her in that case. I'd think he'd want to hide it if it was an accident, not take pictures of her afterward. Doesn't really make sense."

Nodding slowly, he intertwined his fingers, then brought the tips of his index fingers to his lips. "That is very curious indeed. Which leads me to believe it wasn't an accident. What about you, Jennifer? What do you really think?"

I didn't answer, just kept touching the hourglass, stroking the curved glass and smooth wood. Watching the sand trickle down into the lower part. The shimmering grains had an almost hypnotizing effect on me.

"Deep inside, I believe you know better than anyone what the truth is," Dr. Wilkins continued softly. "And it isn't pretty, is it? The question is, can you deal with it? That's why you're really here, isn't it? To let me help you cope with the truth. Tell me the truth, Jennifer. Let me help you deal with it. Put the hourglass back on the desk."

Automatically, I did as he wanted, putting the hourglass

back where I had found it. Then I buried my face in my hands and closed my eyes, hot tears burning the back of the lids. Oh God, my son was a cold-blooded killer... I needed to finally deal with this fact. Dr. Wilkins was *right*. That's why I'd come here today. To deal with it at last. Yes, of course it was so. I simply hadn't known how to cope with it. He would show me how.

I could hear Dr. Wilkins get to his feet and walk over to me. He stopped beside me and I knew what he was holding in his hand—a box of Kleenex.

Steeling myself, I lowered my hands from my face and pulled out a few tissues. I used it to blow my nose, dab at my wet cheeks.

"Take the whole box, Jennifer," Dr. Wilkins said and deposited it in my lap before he went back to have a seat behind his desk.

I used a fresh tissue to dry my eyes that kept filling up with tears.

"Yes, I do think he did it on purpose," I stuttered at last. "I just can't see how someone accidentally pushes someone to their death and then stays silent about it. Acts normally afterward. I remember the night of her death quite well. Shane was his usual happy self. There was nothing about him that suggested he had done some-thing terrible. *Killed* someone. Nothing at all. And I don't understand why he would take those pics afterwards. At least I can't imagine a single *normal* reason for him to do something like that."

"Why would he do something like this?" Dr. Wilkins asked with a grave expression. "I mean, kill someone on purpose if that is indeed what he did. Did he have something against the dead girl?"

"Not as far as I know. To be honest, I thought he really liked her." Another convulsion of sobs went through me that I did my best to suppress. "She's a couple of years older than him. About fourteen. She loved animals and had a special interest in birds. She often went out in the woods to look for them. Study them."

"Okay. Has he ever done anything like this before? Killed on purpose?"

I thought about his question. I was now highly doubting the story Shane had told me about Macy having rabies and attacking him. Yet, even if he had killed the cat on purpose, that was not as bad as having killed another human. Like having shot his own father. But could I really call what Shane had done to his father so many years ago a premeditated murder? Dr. Wilkins obviously knew the story, but he, as everyone else, was under the impression that it had been an accident. I had sworn on it and the police had agreed with me after talking to the child therapist who'd evaluated Shane. It had definitely been an accident. *Of course* it had been an accident only, everyone had agreed in the end. I decided that it wasn't possible for so many people to be wrong. I raised my chin, looked the therapist straight in the eye and said with emphasis, "No, never. This is the first time he's done anything like this. Killed someone in cold blood."

"Well, in that case, you really should take him to a child psychologist trained in dealing with psychotic breaks in children. It does sound like that's what's happened here. We need to figure out what pushed him over the edge so it doesn't happen again. Figure out what made him kill that girl. Did you talk to him about it yet?"

I ran two hands through my hair, pulled it into a low ponytail. "No. I wanted to talk to you first. I honestly don't know how to bring it up to him."

"It might be safer if you do it with a trained professional present."

"I was hoping you could coach me how to talk to him about it. He tends to clam up when he's with a therapist. It took a long time for him to open up after the accident that killed his father. He was devastated."

Dr. Wilkins tilted his head slightly. "Right, the accident that killed his father. I do remember that he'd done something like that, but I can't remember all the details. Would you please refresh my memory?"

I licked my lips that felt uncomfortably dry. "Shane got a hold of his father's gun and it accidentally went off, killing Peter. Shane's father and my husband."

"Ah, yes. I remember now. That must have been incredibly hard on him. I remember how hard it was on you." He smiled with compassion. "Though you did bounce back quicker than I had anticipated, I have to admit."

"Yes, I realized I had to be strong for Shane. It was so hard on both of us. He absolutely hated having to talk about it with a stranger. That's why I thought he might respond better to me. Feel more comfortable opening up. Tell me what happened out there with Alice. He trusts me."

The therapist cocked a brow. "Alice?"

"Yes. That's the name of the girl who died."

Dr. Wilkins inhaled deeply, then cleared his throat. *Uh-oh.* "I know you don't want to hear this, Jennifer, but you really shouldn't bring this up to Shane on your own. It could trigger something in him, make him angry. It's not safe for you, is what I'm trying to tell you. Especially in your current condition." He indicated the crutches with his head. "If he's able to kill a girl who's older than him, he might do something to you. It's best you do it together with a mental health professional. It's too dangerous for you to confront him alone."

I sighed inwardly. I should have known that Dr. Wilkins would say this, insist that I don't bring up the matter to Shane alone. I suddenly regretted having come here. The sad truth was that he was right, but I still didn't like to hear it.

I didn't want my son to be so dangerous I had to fear him.

"What are you thinking?" he asked in that soothing voice that I suddenly found annoying.

I rubbed my fingers against my brows. "That you're right. I shouldn't confront him on my own. It's not wise."

Dr. Wilkins smiled encouragingly. "That's my girl. Do it

together with a trained professional. It'll be best for all parties involved, Shane included. Like I said, he might have just experienced some form of psychotic break. Maybe Alice did something that triggered it. He might be okay if he's put on the right medication. Better at least."

I smiled back at the man, praying that he was right.

15

When I got back home, I called the number on the card that Dr. Wilkins had given me. It was a child psychologist that he recommended, as the one Shane used to see had retired and moved to Florida. A voicemail picked up, so I left a detailed message.

"Who are you calling?" Shane said behind me when I was done, which made me jerk and drop the phone in my hand. It fell to the floor and made a few flip-flops before it stopped moving. Shane immediately squatted and picked it up.

"I'm so sorry, Mom," he said and put it on the desk before me. "I didn't mean to scare you!"

I shook my head and laughed a little. "It's fine. I'm just a little jumpy these days. I didn't hear you come home. I called a doctor I might need to see." I couldn't make myself tell him that he would also need to see the doctor in question; that, in fact, it was the reason I'd called her.

"Oh. Are you still feeling sick?" He gazed at me with a concerned expression.

I shrugged and waved a dismissive hand in the air. "Yeah, but it's nothing serious. I'm already feeling better."

"Are you sure? I don't want to lose you too. You're all I have left, Mom. Promise me you'll never leave me."

He gazed at me with those teal-colored, clear eyes, blinking a couple of times, looking so sad and helpless suddenly that I felt a pang of pain in my heart. A wave of guilt rode through me. What had I been thinking? That Shane might hurt me? How could I think that even for one second? He had never ever shown an inclination of wanting to hurt me in any way, quite the opposite. He was a good boy, someone who loved to help others. I'd seen that side of him often over the years, and especially after my car accident. He'd been indispensable around the house.

My mother had offered to stay with me, but Shane had been so helpful every day that I'd told her it was completely unnecessary.

I smiled and ran a knuckle over his soft cheek. "I promise I'll be around for many more years, honey. You won't get rid of me that easily."

It dawned on me that this was a good moment to ask him about the pics in his phone. Well, as good as it would ever get to bring up such a thing. The suddenly sunny weather outside the window in my study further brightened my mind, making me feel more optimistic about the outcome. For sure it would turn out there was a reasonable explanation for what those pics were doing there, just like there had been a reasonable explanation for him attacking Macy. There was no way he'd be able to fake all those scratches and bites on his body! Why had that even occurred to me?

I had spent the morning feeling convinced that he'd marked himself to make it seem like Macy had attacked him. That he had just swallowed the pain this had caused, added scratch after scratch, a bite here and a bite there. For all I knew, he might even have used the cat's own claws to create more realistic scratches. Anything seemed possible now.

The fact of the matter was that no one had taken a close look at the marks until much later, when most were halfway healed already.

Well, he obviously didn't give himself those marks, I told myself now. Macy did.

I placed a hand on his arm. "Shane. I need to talk to you about something."

"What is it?" He looked suddenly worried.

"Why are there pictures of Alice Tate lying dead on the ground in your phone?" I blurted before I could change my mind. There, I'd said it at last. Holding my breath, I watched his reaction carefully. First, all he did was stare at me as the seconds ticked by. *Tic, toc. Tic, toc. Tic, toc.* My heart picked up speed and goosebumps formed on my arms.

Why was he looking at me like that?

He just kept staring and staring at me, his face dark. I swallowed hard, regretting not having followed Dr. Wilkins's suggestion. *Why didn't I listen?*

Then, as suddenly as his face had darkened, he piped in a small voice: "Am I in trouble?"

A beat went by, then the words streamed out of his mouth: "I was out walking in the woods and saw her there on the ground. Dead and all bloody. It was *super creepy*. I wanted to rush home and tell everyone, but I was afraid I would forget where I found her or that people would think I'd made it all up, so I took the pics. A lot of them. Maybe I got carried away, I can't remember, I was so shocked. I also took some pics of the area. That's all. I *promise.* Then, when I hurried back home, it hit me that people might think that *I* had something to do with her death, so I decided not to say anything. She was dead anyway and I didn't want to get in trouble! Am I in trouble, Mom? Was that why you called that doctor? It was, wasn't it?" He spoke faster and faster, his voice becoming increasingly shrieky. He seemed on the verge of having a panic attack, so I grabbed both his arms and told him to calm down, to take a deep breath. I told him he wasn't in trouble at all.

"I'm glad you told me what you did," I continued at the same time as I searched my memory of other pics in his phone that featured the surroundings. I relaxed when I remembered that I had in fact seen several of those as well. Shane must be telling me the truth then. I embraced him hard and whispered, "I understand that you were scared, honey. It's okay. Nothing bad will happen to you. It's true that I was a little worried when I saw those photos in your phone. I even went to see Dr. Wilkins to talk about it."

Removing myself from him, I chuckled and smiled warmly at him. "Which was completely unnecessary, I now realize. I should've known all along that there was a perfectly reasonable explanation for those photos. I should have known all along that you had nothing to do with her death!" I rolled my eyes at myself.

He stared at me, his eyes round and big and terrified. "You told Dr. Wilkins I had *done* something to Alice? Like, pushed her or something? Why would you do that? I would never hurt Alice! Alice was my friend!"

"Shhh," I told Shane and squeezed his upper arms firmly. "I made a mistake and I'm sorry. It will all be okay."

"Maybe he thinks I killed Alice and tells the police! Then I'll go to *jail*. I don't want to go to jail!"

"No, honey, that won't happen." I tried to hug him again, but he pushed me away.

"How can you be so sure? I don't want to go to jail!"

"Because I'll tell him it was all a big misunderstanding, okay? Then he'll have no reason to tell the police." I didn't see the need to get into specifics with Shane, that mental health professionals had a confidentiality obligation toward their patients. They could only break that if they had reason to believe someone was in danger, children or elderly people were abused, or they were subpoenaed by the court to speak. So far, Dr. Wilkins and I hadn't determined that Shane posed a danger to anyone but perhaps me. Which I would tell him he could forget about. All was fine with Shane.

"Do you understand what I'm saying, honey?" I asked him, my hands still on his shoulders.

He looked down at the floor. "Yes, I do."

"Good. You probably should delete those photos, though. If people see them, they might get the wrong idea. It's not smart to have them in your phone like that." *You even had your own mom fooled,* I thought but didn't say. That would likely reignite his panic.

"Okay, I'll delete them." He raised his chin and gazed straight into my eyes, smiling now. Relief was written all over his face. "Thanks for believing me, Mom."

"Of course I believe you," I said and hugged him hard and this time he let me. It was only as I squeezed his lanky body toward mine that it struck me—why had Shane gone into the woods in the first place that day...?

16

I remembered then that the weather had been beautiful that May day, warm and sunny after a string of rainy, unseasonably cool ones. Considering the drastic change in weather, it wasn't strange actually if my son had decided to take a walk in the woods. He had always liked to be outdoors, especially in the summer, and clear days like that one were great for taking pictures.

I let go of him and laughed inwardly at my neurotic ways. *There you go again, Jennifer!* As it turned out, not only was it perfectly okay to ask Shane about those photos, but he also had a good explanation as to why they had been in his phone. When I saw the gruesome images, I'd totally forgotten about the other photos of the surroundings that had preceded them. Which was understandable given how upset I'd been.

Well, when I call Dr. Wilkins and explain to him what really happened out there, he'd understand.

"Promise me that you'll delete those photos, okay?" I told Shane, still holding his shoulders. "If someone else sees them, they could get the wrong idea."

"You mean like you did?" Shane asked with a lopsided smile.

I inhaled and exhaled. "Yes. Sorry, I'm only human. Can you forgive me, honey?"

He nodded and smiled. "Yes. I forgive you, Mom."

"Good. What time is it?" I looked around the office for a clock. I spotted the clock radio on a side table. It was four p.m. I turned back to Shane. "Don't you have soccer training at 4: 30?"

He grimaced. "Do I have to go? I hate playing soccer."

"Yes, honey. You do. You begged for me to sign you up for this class and you've only been twice. Give it a few more tries before you bail on it. It might turn out you'll love it!"

He rolled his eyes. "I highly doubt that."

"Well, you'll have to go at least one more time. If you absolutely hate it after today, we'll reconsider, okay?"

"Okay. Thanks, Mom." He swiveled around and left the office.

I resumed working on a manuscript that I'd been editing when Shane entered the room all of a sudden. Or trying to edit—I hadn't gotten much done today. I wanted to call Dr. Wilkins right away to tell him that I had been wrong in assuming Alice had died because of Shane. But I didn't want to call before Shane had left the apartment. Overhearing my conversation with Dr. Wilkins would likely only serve to upset him, and I had upset him enough today.

He called out a loud goodbye and left the apartment ten minutes later. I could hear the front door open and shut, but just to be on the safe side, I didn't pick up my phone and call until I could see Shane coming out of the apartment building. I didn't want to take any risks, him suddenly coming back when I was in the middle of a conversation.

Dr. Wilkins picked up on the fourth ring.

"Hello."

"Hi, Dr. Wilkins, it's Jennifer Hanson."

"Hi, Jennifer. How are you today? Did you get a chance to call the child psychologist?"

"Yes, I did, but I only left a voicemail."

"She'll get back to you soon."

"About that. I actually just spoke to Shane about the photos."

"You did? How did he react?" Dr. Wilkins sounded wary.

"It turns out that he only bumped into her as he was walking around in the woods, taking pics. Or her body, I should say. When he saw her on the ground and realized that she was dead, he took pics of the environment, as well as of her body. He didn't know what else to do when it dawned on him that he had no idea where he was. He was worried he'd forget where he'd seen her or that people would think he was just making it up. He thought the pics would help the police find her quicker, as someone was bound to recognize the area. I actually saw the pics of the environment, but I totally forgot about them when I saw the ones of Alice. Then, as he was on his way back, he freaked out that people would think he had something to do with her accident, so that's why he never said anything about them when he got back home. Which is perfectly understandable. I mean, his own *mother* thought so. I feel so ashamed now. I, if anyone, should know that my son isn't capable of killing someone in cold blood, right?"

"Um, yes, that's true. So you no longer believe he had anything to do with it then?"

"I don't. I spoke to him about it for a while and I'm convinced he was telling me the truth."

"Okay. Well, I still think it's a good idea if Shane sees the child psychologist. Running into the dead girl, his friend, and worrying about people thinking that he had some-thing to do with it must have been a traumatic experience for him. He really should talk to a professional about it."

I thought about what Dr. Wilkins had just suggested. "Hmm. Yes, that might be a good idea. I didn't think about it in those terms."

"I understand. But you see why it's important then?"

"I sure do. I will absolutely make an appointment with Dr. Roth as soon as she returns my call."

"That's good. And when am I seeing you again? We never made another appointment."

"Right. You know what? For now I think I'm good. I really just wanted to discuss that matter with you, and we solved it."

"Oh, okay. Well, let me know what happens with Shane and Dr. Roth. I think she will be great for him."

"I will definitely be in touch. Thanks again for the referral."

17

When Shane returned home three hours later, he was hungry and grumpy. I had already prepared dinner, meatloaf with mashed potatoes, gravy, and cranberries, which was one of Shane's favorite meals. It never ceased to amaze me how much of it he could get into his skinny body. Already seated at the dinner table, I poured some OJ for him in the glass next to his food.

"How was it?" I asked when he marched into the kitchen and plopped down on the chair on the other side of the table.

"It sucked. I *told* you I hate soccer." He stabbed a piece of meatloaf with his fork, used the knife to shove some mashed and gravy on top of it, then a few cranberries. The whole mishmash went into his gaping mouth and he barely chewed the food before he swallowed. He repeated the process, loading more into his mouth.

"Take it easy, honey," I said and had a sip of my straw-berry-tasting sparkling water, a new offering from Pelle-grino, my favorite brand of water. "If you keep that up, you might choke."

"No, I know what I'm doing," he muttered in between forkfuls.

"That's good, because I would hate it if I had to resusci-tate you while on the crutches. It's not exactly easy to move around."

He didn't answer, just kept eating. I could feel him fuming, how upset he was.

"What happened that made you so upset, Shane?" I asked after a couple of minutes of tense silence.

He glanced at me, scowling. "One of the players on the other team tripped me and I almost broke my ankle."

"Really? That's not good. I'm so sorry to hear that. I didn't notice you limping when you came over to the table."

"That's because you had your back to me. I'm limping plenty. I might need your crutches to be able to walk tomorrow," he added dramatically.

I couldn't help but chuckle a little. "You're welcome to borrow them from me. I don't really need them when I'm at home writing. I can use the cane." My mother had dropped off her own mother's old cane for me to use.

He glared at me, the fork full of meatloaf and gravy-drenched mash frozen in midair. "It's not funny. It hurts!"

I forced myself to get serious. "I'm sorry, honey. I know it must hurt. Thank God it wasn't worse. You could have broken your leg like I did."

"Yeah, I know. I'm never again playing any stupid sport. It's such a waste of *time.*"

"And you don't have to either." I smiled at him. "Didn't I tell you that if you didn't like it after today, you could stop going?"

He huffed. "Yeah, I'm definitely not going back there again. I hate those idiots."

I cocked a brow at him. "You hate all of them?"

"Yeah." He avoided my gaze.

"Why is that?"

He shrugged. "They are just idiots." He shoved more food into his mouth and chewed for a little longer before swallowing this time.

"Well, you'll never have to see those idiots again, either." It dawned on me that he might have to see at least some of them in school still. "At least not during soccer practice. You've made it crystal clear to me that soccer is not for you." I contemplated bringing up the fact that I wanted him to see the therapist I had called, but I figured tonight was not the right time for that. I had the distinct feeling that Shane wouldn't be happy to hear I wanted him to see another shrink. He'd never been a fan of them. He would also realize that I had lied to him in regard to the doctor I'd left a message for. I had no doubt he'd remember the name of the doctor, as he was not only smart, but also had a very good memory. He wouldn't like me having lied to him.

He didn't answer, just kept eating his food until there was nothing left on the plate.

"Do you want more food?" I asked him. I wasn't even half done with my own meal.

"No, thank you. Can I be excused?"

"Sure. Unless you want to have some ice cream for dessert? I have chunky chocolate Haagen-Dazs in the freezer." I wiggled my brows at him suggestively.

The sound of anything sweet usually cheered him up when he was in a pissy mood like tonight.

"Nah, I'm stuffed. And I have to finish my homework."

"Oh, okay. Go ahead and do that then."

A little deflated, I watched him push out his chair and grab his plate, silverware, and empty glass. He brought it over to the sink in the kitchen counter, limping lightly. After he had rinsed off his stuff and stuck it in the dishwasher, he left the kitchen and walked down the hallway and into his room at the other end of the apartment.

I remained at the dinner table, eating my dinner. Or trying to eat might be a more accurate way of describing what I was doing; mostly, I was just shifting the food around on my plate. I wasn't very hungry this evening.

It didn't take long before it dawned on me why that was. I was suddenly filled with thoughts of Peter, and it made my stomach turn. More than six years had passed since his death, but to me it still felt like it had all happened yesterday, the pain of missing him was so all-encompassing. That is, when I allowed myself to think of my dead husband. I dealt with his memory by boxing in my feelings, keeping them separate from the rest of my brain. Most of the time that approach worked just fine. It had been the way Shane had limped over to the kitchen counter that had triggered the thoughts of Peter tonight, though.

Unlike his son, Peter had been a rather athletic man, who liked to play soccer and run in the woods. Where we'd lived in the edges of Long Island, there was a large park in which he had loved to run most days of the week. Once, when Shane was only four, he had played a game of soccer with some friends in that park. His team had won because Peter had scored the winning shot, but in order to do so, he had also tripped and twisted his ankle. It had taken him several days to recover during which he had moaned and complained worse than his toddler son did. Shane making his way over to the dishwasher had been just the way Peter had done it when he'd cleaned his side of the dinner table.

I pushed away my plate and limped over to the cupboard by the fridge and pulled out a bottle of California Cabernet Sauvignon. I didn't drink alcohol very often. The wine bottles in my house could remain there for many months, years even, before I got to them.

Usually, I only had some wine when I had friends over for dinner, or when the longing for my husband was too strong. Getting a little drunk was the most efficient way to soothe the pain. Tonight was definitely one of those nights when I could use some wine therapy.

I found a corkscrew in one of the drawers next to the sink and uncorked the bottle. Then I got a wine glass from a cupboard and filled it up with the thick, dark red liquid. I brought the bottle with me and walked into the living room where I curled up in a corner of the couch. Looking around the room, I searched for Macy only to remember that she was no longer with us. A horrific image of my son stabbing the cat in the country house flashed through my mind, but I managed to make it disintegrate before it could take root and add to my misery. I had nearly succeeded in convincing myself that Macy had just run away, not gotten rabies and turned crazy, forcing Shane to kill her. I much preferred the made-up version to the truth. I attributed the fact that Macy had only been with us a little over a year to my having dealt with losing her so well. There hadn't been enough time for me to get attached to her. Well, that and the fact that I had been in the car accident had forced me to think of other things but dead pets.

I wasn't in the mood to get another cat quite yet, though. Quite frankly, I wasn't sure I would get one before I was living on my own, and I couldn't figure out why I felt that way. Perhaps it had something to do with Shane not being as much of an animal lover as I was, in particular of cats.

While I had grown up with both cats and dogs and couldn't imagine a childhood without animals, neither Shane nor his father had been keen on pets. While Peter had been alive, we hadn't had any animals, and it was only because a friend's new boyfriend was allergic to cats that we had adopted Macy, a fully grown cat.

Now that I thought about it, Shane and Macy had never gotten along well. She had never leaped into his lap and curled up the way she had into mine. As a matter of fact, she tended to avoid Shane and Shane her. He rarely petted the cat, never played with it. I had asked him once if the cat bothered him, and he had just shrugged and shaken his head.

Since I found the gray and white ball of fur such great company when I felt lonely and watched TV in the evenings, I hadn't thought much about it. Maybe there had been more animosity between Shane and Macy than I had suspected. If that was so, it would explain why Shane had reacted so strongly, so violently to Macy attacking him. It would also explain why Macy had launched herself on Shane and not me. The rabies had just served to unleash what was already brewing inside that furry little body.

Poor Macy, I thought and my heart ached for the animal almost as much as it did for how Peter had died.

I emptied my glass and filled it up again. I had a feeling that tonight I'd empty the wine bottle in record time.

18

The phone rang when I was in the middle of the last chapter of the book I was editing. I was so into the story that the sound of the ringing was jarring to my ears. Shuddering, I looked around the home office to see where I'd put my cell phone.

I was fairly convinced the call had gone to voicemail by the time I found it under some papers at the other side of the desk. It hadn't.

I pressed the Talk key and put the phone to my ear.

"Hello?"

"Hi, my name is Dr. Karen Roth and I'd like to speak to Jennifer Hanson."

"That's me." As I said those words, I quickly searched my mind for who Dr. Roth was. I knew I had heard the name before, but I couldn't remember where or why. At the same time as the woman's comforting voice explained that I had left a message for her a few days earlier, it came to me. She was the child psychologist Dr. Wilkins wanted Shane to see.

"Oh yes, that's right," I said and straightened in the chair as though the woman could see me. "I did do that. I think, at the moment, we won't be doing any therapy. My son and I figured out what the problem was, and he's doing much better actually. I thought about Dr. Wilkins's suggestion that Shane could use therapy to deal with having bumped into a dead person. I respectfully disagree it would be wise. I think having him talk about the issue again might trigger more trauma in him. See, I have a Master's degree in psychology, so I'm not completely imagining this. Sometimes it's better to just let things be."

"Oh, okay. Well, if anything changes, you have my number."

"I do have that. I'll definitely get back to you if things change with him."

I thanked her for calling, then hung up the call.

I really did feel it was a bad idea for Shane to be discussing what had happened out in the woods. Sometimes, you really did make things worse by talking about them over and over when what someone needed was just to forget. Children were more resilient than people gave them credit for, especially mental health professionals. Shane would be fine on his own. Well, under my guidance.

I returned to my work and had started on another manuscript by the time Shane returned from school.

The next couple of weeks moved along without anything interesting or unusual happening. My leg kept improving and I felt stronger. Fall fell over Northeast America at a steady pace, the days getting shorter and rain hitting the ground more than I would like, the skies gray and filled with giant clouds. Shane's ankle healed quickly and he walked normally now. Instead of playing soccer, he had taken up playing the guitar with a man who gave lessons at his house. I thought it was a good idea, albeit a bit strange. Shane had never really been into playing instruments, but I was willing to give it a go if he thought he might enjoy it. Anything that would get him away from the computer and social media I encouraged.

It wasn't until a Monday in early November that I found out what had happened to Dr. Wilkins. I read about it in the Uptown section of the NY Daily News.

Someone had broken into the psychologist's Upper East Side apartment and stabbed him to death in the middle of the night. The police were still on the lookout for the perpetrator. It appeared like the motive for the break-in had been to kill the doctor, not to rob the apartment, as that seemed untouched.

A chill went through me as I kept reading the short article in the middle of the paper. The coroner estimated the murder to have taken place on Thursday night a week ago. The reason the body had been found four days later, on a Sunday afternoon, was because the therapist was single and it had been a weekend. The patients he was supposed to see on Friday hadn't notified the police until Sunday that it appeared Dr. Wilkins was missing.

I stared at the words in the article, not actually seeing them any longer. Poor Dr. Wilkins. Why would anyone want to kill Dr. Wilkins? Could it be one of his patients who'd had a grudge against him? It had to be. People who dealt with mentally ill people must have a few of those in their lives, just like lawyers and detectives. Over the years, the few probably became several. Based on the framed certifications behind his chair in his office, Dr. Wilkins had been practicing psychology for decades.

I checked the article again to see if the name of the detective on the case was mentioned. I really wanted to talk to him or her, see if I could be of help.

There wasn't a name in the article, so I had to call the police and ask them to find out for me.

Five minutes later I had learned that the detective handling the case was Detective Ivan Morales. The operator had given me all his contact information. She told me he would be happy to talk to me.

I called him and he picked up on the second ring.

"Ivan Morales," a male, steady-sounding voice said with just a trace of an accent.

"Hello, my name is Jennifer Hanson and I was one of Dr. Wilkins's patients. I was told you're handling his murder case?"

"Yes, I am. How can I help you?"

"Well, I was just calling to see if I could assist in the investigation. I knew Dr. Wilkins well. I used to see him a lot a few years ago, and I also went to see him a few weeks ago for a session."

"Okay, thank you. Do you have any reason to believe someone would want to see Dr. Wilkins dead?"

"Um, not off the top of my head. Do you have any suspects?"

"No, not at the moment. But the investigation has barely started. We're certainly going to go through the doctor's patient load to see if there's anyone in particular we should consider a threat. We do believe this was personal. So you can't think of anyone like that right now?"

"Unfortunately not, but I'll keep thinking and maybe I'll come up with someone. I just saw the article about Dr. Wilkins's murder in the paper, and I felt compelled to do something. It's so awful. He was such a nice, kind man, a great therapist. I know he dealt with a lot of crazy people, but I still can't see why anyone would want to kill him."

"Yes, he had a good reputation in his field. Well, thanks for calling. If you do think of anything you believe might be helpful, please don't hesitate to call me again. I'm sorry, but could you please tell me your name again?"

"Of course. It's Jennifer Hanson." I gave him my phone number as well, then we disconnected the call.

I felt a little silly having contacted the detective now. I hadn't been particularly helpful, had I? Why had I thought I would make a difference in the investigation? It wasn't like I knew what was going on with Dr. Wilkins's other patients. I was well aware that he wasn't allowed to discuss other patients, so what had I been thinking? Detective Morales had been exceedingly polite with me when he must have thought I was only wasting his time.

I shook my head and went to fill up my coffee cup.

19

November 15th was Shane's thirteenth birthday, which fell on a Saturday this year. During the day, I had taken him and three friends of his to McDonalds, which happened to be Shane's favorite place to eat. A few hours later, when the celebration was over, I took him shopping for a new laptop like I had promised he would get for his next birthday.

We found the right one for him after only half an hour, a MacBook Pro on which he could play his video games as well as edit all his photos. I had known all along that was what he had wanted, so I took him straight to the store where there was a sale on all Mac computers.

When we got back home later, Shane and I had dinner. This was the seventh birthday we spent without Peter joining us. Even though it had been many years now since he'd died, I couldn't help but miss him as much as ever. The sound of his deep voice. The way he smelled faintly of soap and aftershave. His distinctly male, protective presence.

"What's wrong, Mom?" Shane asked, looking at me thoughtfully with those pretty eyes of his, blinking slowly.

I shook my head, snapping back to reality. I had allowed myself to float away on cushy dream clouds filled with Peter, what he might have been like today had he been alive. Would he have grays in his thick head of dark brown hair? He'd be forty-two now, so it was possible. If that were the case, it would only have made him more handsome, lent him an air of distinction.

I reached out and ran a knuckle over Shane's cheek. "I'm sorry, honey. I just got to thinking of—" I caught myself before I could spell out what had gone through my head, tell Shane just how much I missed his dad. All that would accomplish would be for Shane to feel worse than he already did about what he had done to his father.

He had been six and a half at the time of the shooting, and from what I had been able to understand, he had very strong memories of the event. There was no need to increase the pain and guilt associated with those by bringing up Peter's name and how I wished he was with us today. According to the therapist Shane had been seeing, Shane experienced lots of guilt for what he had done.

"—of the latest book I'm editing," I finished the sentence. "It's been on my mind for days. It's so very good! I think this author might well have a bestseller on her hands."

Shane nodded. "What's it about?"

"It's a thriller about a man who feels trapped in a loveless marriage, and how he acts out because of this. Not a children's book exactly," I added with a half smile. Lovestruck had expanded recently, adding a thriller line.

"Does he kill people?" Shane asked, looking sincerely interested in the answer.

I stared at him. "Um, yeah, in fact he does. What made you think of that?"

He shrugged. "Don't know. Does he see a therapist about feeling trapped in his marriage?"

"Yes, he does. How did you figure that out?"

He grinned big. "I'm a genius, Mom. Did you already forget that?"

I laughed. "No, of course not."

The grin on Shane's face disappeared as quickly as it had gotten there. "Did he kill his own therapist?"

I could feel my eyebrows furrow. "Why do you ask that?"

"Because therapists can be real annoying sometimes."

I tilted my head. "They can? How so?"

Shane looked away from me and out the window that displayed a dreary sky filled with rain-heavy clouds. "They ask so many questions. Get mixed up in stuff that's really none of their business."

I stared at him in silence for a few seconds. "It sounds like you have experience with this behavior. Are you telling me your therapist did this to you?"

Shane insisted on glancing out the window.

I grabbed his wrist. "Shane. Please look at me."

Reluctantly, he turned his head slowly toward me. "What part?"

Irritation grew inside me. Why was he acting so weird? So flippant? It wasn't like him. I inhaled quietly through my nostrils to calm down; snapping at Shane didn't improve any situation. I needed to remain composed. "Did your therapist ask you too many questions?"

"Sometimes." He shrugged noncommittally.

"You know that that's their job, don't you? To ask a lot of questions, some of which might make the patient uncomfortable."

"Yeah, I know." Shane shoved food onto his fork with the help of his knife. "But it's not their job to get mixed up in stuff that's really not their business." He stuck the fork into his mouth at the same time as he held my gaze, daring me to challenge his statement.

"Why do you bring this up, Shane? Did this happen to you?"

As usual, he swallowed after only having chewed his food a few times. "Yes. But I took care of it, so no harm was done." He gave a pleasant smile.

It was suddenly hard for me to breathe, my throat got so

constricted. Something about this was not right, but I couldn't put my finger on exactly what it was. All I knew was that it was bothering me very much.

I licked my lips, then cleared my throat. "You took care of it. What's that supposed to mean?"

"That everything will be fine in the end. No one will get in trouble."

I put down my own silverware, pushed my plate away, and placed my elbows on the table. "Please tell me exactly what you're referring to, Shane."

He smiled at me. "Don't worry so much, Mom. I was only speaking in general terms. Can I be excused? I'm sorta tired. I wanna go lie down. I don't have room for more dessert." We had eaten double ice cream sundaes at McDonalds earlier, but I had also baked a cake for dinner. Shane loved sweet stuff and today I would allow him to eat as much of it as he wanted. "We can eat it tomorrow."

I fixed him with my gaze, debating whether I should press him on what he'd said, demand more specifics. But I was suddenly overcome by a wave of exhaustion. It had been a long day and I wasn't in the mood to discuss this any further. I was probably just overreacting like I so often did when it came to Shane and his sometime curious statements.

So I patted his arm and said, "Sure, honey. Go lie down and get some rest. Then we'll watch a movie together. Your pick."

20

I didn't sleep well at all that night. I had strange dreams in which Peter visited me. He was telling me to stay strong for Shane, never to forget that it wasn't Shane's fault he was born with psychopathic tendencies. Nor was it our son's fault that his uncle had sexually abused him, potentially unleashed dark forces within him. I needed to do everything in my power to ensure those forces never surfaced, quell the ones that had. Reverse them. Destroy and replace them with positive ones.

When I woke up in the morning, by myself several minutes before the alarm went off at seven, I was sweaty and shivering, I was so cold. Was I coming down with something? That would be annoying, as I really didn't have time to be sick. I was behind in the editing and had already been given a warning by my boss that I had to do a better job meeting my deadlines. I placed a hand on my forehead to gauge if it was hot. It wasn't, instead it felt cool and clammy.

Stretching my limbs in bed, I checked if my joints hurt or were sore. They weren't. I swallowed and my throat didn't hurt, either. Except for my left leg, which knee was still stiff in the mornings, nothing felt wrong with me. That knee felt especially stiff when it was rainy and very chilly outside like lately, atypical fall weather for this part of the country. Yes, I was fine.

I relaxed and allowed myself a moment to stare up into the ceiling while pondering my dreams. If nothing else they were timely, because, as I had gone to bed last night, thoughts of what Shane had brought up at dinner had continued to float around in my head. The more I considered what he'd said, the worse I'd felt. I couldn't shake the sensation that Shane was hiding something from me. What I had no idea, but he was up to something and I didn't like it.

Well, he is a teenager now, Jennifer, I reminded myself. Teenagers are by definition unpredictable and full of mischief. Very smart ones like my son would surely turn out to be more than a handful. Yes, I sighed. It'd be a rough few years, but somehow we'd get through them together. We'd just take one day at a time. I only wished that Peter was with us still to help me deal with what was to come. It would have been so much easier, and I wouldn't have felt so lonely, not to mention stressed out at times. I missed him so.

I pushed myself out of bed before feelings of sadness took over, making me stay where I was and feel sorry for myself and how my life had ended up. I had to stay strong for Shane. Take care of him properly.

An hour later, he and I had had breakfast and he had gone off to school. I was seated at my desk in the home study, getting ready to read one of the manuscripts I had been sent and was overdue.

Another hour went by and I had only gotten to the sixth page. At that rate, I'd finish the book in a month instead of in four days, which was my usual pace. Not acceptable, especially not this week. I should be working twice as fast.

Even so, I decided that I could no longer put off what I had secretly wanted to do since I took a seat at the desk that morning and placed my cell phone next to the laptop. I reached for the cell and found Detective Morales's number somewhere in the call log. Calling it, I placed the phone to my ear.

He answered on the second ring. "Ivan Morales."

"Good morning, Detective, this is Jennifer Hanson. We spoke about a week ago in regard to Dr. Wilkins's murder. I was one of his patients."

"Ah, yes, I remember. How are you, Ms. Hanson?"

"I'm well, thank you. I was just calling to see how the investigation was going. Did you arrest anyone yet?"

"Unfortunately not. As a matter of fact, we're struggling to come up with good leads. It's not good. Do you have any for me?" He sounded like he expected I did.

"Um, no, I don't think so. I just can't stop thinking about how sad it is that he's gone, and in such a brutal manner. He didn't deserve to go that way. He was such a nice man. Such a good therapist. I miss him so. I think I mentioned that I had a session with him shortly before he was murdered?"

"Yes, you did mention that." He cleared his throat. "You don't have to answer this, Ms. Hanson, but if I may, why did you see Dr. Wilkins? What was your issue?"

"I...I was having some difficulties with my son. He's been a handful lately." The images of dead Alice in my son's phone flashed through my mind, making my stomach twist with discomfort. I wasn't about to bring up those to this detective. Part of me knew that I probably should, but another bigger part, knew that might get Shane in trouble. The last thing I wanted was for the authorities to take a closer look at my son, figure out what was going on with his brain, never mind all the trauma he'd been through in his formative years. The fact that he had shot his own father.

"So you went to see Dr. Wilkins to discuss your son then?" the detective asked.

"No, not exactly. More how to deal with my son." I closed my eyes and cursed myself. I could tell that Detective Morales had perked up considerably, liking the way this conversation was going, and that he wasn't about to let up anytime soon. What had I been thinking when I had called him this afternoon? I should have known this was how it would end up. At the very least, I should have hung up the second I found out they were still lacking leads and just thanked him for the update. I had craved an update.

"Tell me about your son, Ms. Hanson. How old is he?"

"Um, twelve. No, wait, he turned thirteen yesterday as a matter of fact."

"Ah, a young teen then. What kind of problems are you having with him?"

"He, ah, he just does reckless stuff sometimes and I'm a widow, so I find it hard to deal with him sometimes. That's all. Nothing that serious really."

"I see. I have a meeting I have to attend to in a couple of minutes, so I'm afraid I have to get going. If you have anything else you want to talk about, you're welcome to give me a call later. I'll be available then."

"Oh, of course. Thanks, I think I'm good. I just wanted to see how the investigation was going. I'm so sorry you don't have any leads and that I haven't been able to give you any, either."

"No worries. Goodbye, Ms. Hanson."

"Goodbye."

As soon as I had disconnected the call, I stuck my fist into my mouth and bit hard into the knuckles. Oh God, I was such a fucking *idiot*. What the hell was I doing, calling this detective over and over with questions about Wilkins's murder? Why had it been so damned important for me to find out the status of the investigation? If he didn't think so before, Detective Morales surely suspected *now* that I had something to do with the murder. I or, worse, Shane.

If he was a halfway decent detective, he would look into who I was and who my son was. He had my name and phone number, so that should be a piece of cake. And when he took a closer look at our history, he would find out that not only had my husband been shot to death, but the shooter had been our only child. It had been all over the news for over a week around the time it had happened, the media and gun control lobbyists making the most of it. Detective Morales had likely read and/or heard about it and would instantly remember details of the case. The fact that my son's name hadn't been mentioned due to him being a minor didn't matter; Detective Morales no doubt had access to the police reports filed in the case. Combine that with the fact that I had just handed him fresh information regarding how hard it was for me to deal with my son—so hard I needed the advice and assistance of a shrink—he would be stupid not to consider me or Shane for Dr. Wilkins's murder. He was in desperate need for leads, so even a farfetched lead such as this one would do. Because it had to be farfetched, right? I couldn't imagine that anything at the crime scene suggested that a kid had killed Dr. Wilkins.

I highly doubted Morales had a meeting he had to go to. No, it had surely been an excuse so that he could get to the bottom of who this crazy woman with the difficult son was as quickly as possible.

I wanted to pace the room to release all the nervous

energy building inside me, but it would be too hard with the cane I had recently graduated to. I contented myself with drumming my fingers on the desk. Damn it. What the hell should I do? If he wanted to, Detective Morales would be able to get access to Dr. Wilkins's notes for our last session. He could subpoena them through a judge. I didn't know if Wilkins kept detailed notes of his sessions, all I knew was that he liked to jot down basic stuff on his yellow legal pad during our conversations. This meant the detective would be able to figure out that I had worried about my son having killed yet another person. First his father, then Alice Tate. All that was needed to arrive at that conclusion was for there to be a note that said something along the lines of "pics of dead girl in son's phone". I doubted I would be able to keep it together was I forced to talk more about those pics; for sure the police would question me about them.

I didn't want the detective to talk to Shane either. He didn't need the trauma of police interrogating him about murder. Who knew how insensitive they'd be with him, even with me being present? He was just a boy and had been traumatized enough in his life. What if an interrogation would push him over the edge and be the straw that broke the camel's back? Worse, what if Shane said something that incriminated him? I wouldn't be able to control everything he said or did during the interrogation. We didn't have the money to hire a great lawyer to be present, so it could very well happen. Then Shane might get arrested and placed in a cell overnight with hardcore criminals. I was pretty sure he'd get treated as an adult due to the seriousness of the crime even though he was only 13. Staying the night in a prison cell full of crooks would be very bad for him. Did I really want to risk that happening? No, I didn't.

I ran a hand through my hair. What the hell should I *do?* I needed to make sure the cop didn't get a chance to talk to Shane or me in depth. But how would I do that? The only way would be for us to be physically unavailable. Hide somewhere. Run away. But if we did that, wasn't that the same as admitting guilt? If I were in the detective's shoes, I would think so.

Well, maybe I could call Detective Morales from wherever we were and plead with him, explain to him why I needed to protect my son from additional trauma in his life. Explain to him that we were both innocent, that he was wasting his time focusing on us. I couldn't risk putting Shane through more trauma. He was barely hanging on as it was. He needed space to heal. Shane needed lots of love, positivity, and a structured environment to heal. Or I could tell the detective all that in a letter. Yes, a letter was better. I'd explain everything to Detective Morales in a letter.

We'll run away then, Shane and I. How much time did we have before the police showed up at our door and demanded to speak to me and Shane? I thought that we had at least another day. Detective Morales had no reason to believe I would be hard to get a hold of given that I had called him twice and freely offered information about myself and Shane. What normal person who'd done something bad—or had knowledge of someone else's bad behavior—would do that? No one. That meant that I didn't have to rush to Shane's school and pull him out and take him with me somewhere. I could wait until he came home later.

I sighed heavily. Where should we go, though? Upstate, to my parents' country house perhaps? No, that wasn't good. Too many people knew us there. My parents and friends would likely cave under pressure and reveal potential hiding spots such as the country house.

We had to go somewhere no one could easily figure out. And once we were there, I would contact Detective Morales and explain why I had felt I'd had no choice but to run away. It really was the only way I could protect my son from more harm.

He didn't deserve to experience more than he already had.

21

W hen Shane came home several hours later, I had already written the letter to Detective Morales in which I had thoroughly explained why I was taking Shane away. Why I saw no other choice. I would leave it with my mom and have her give it to him in person. If I mailed it to the police station, it might get lost and I didn't feel like wasting more time digging up his home address. I had already tried and couldn't find it. The NYPD had likely made it hard to find on purpose.

"Hi Mom, what are you doing?" my son asked, sticking his head into the home office.

I signed the letter and looked up. "I'm just writing a document, honey. How was school?"

He shrugged lightly. "Boring."

I don't know what it was, but as I was about to tell Shane what I had planned to say, that we were taking a trip somewhere, something made me pause. No matter how much I tried, my tongue refused to form the words. Maybe I was acting crazy here. Was it really the right thing to do to run away with Shane? It would never work, would it? Wouldn't I just make everything worse for him? Being on the run wasn't exactly the structured, stable environment he needed to develop into a good person. And I still hadn't figured out where we would go. Where the hell would we go? And how long would we be gone? I couldn't just count on the police finding the killer in the next week or so. What if they didn't find him or her? That meant we would have to be on the run forever, and that was definitely not a good option.

What if Detective Morales was a crappy investigator? In that case, he wouldn't put two and two together like I'd feared. That was just as likely, wasn't it? Okay, fine, maybe not. I'd heard somewhere that the NYPD was a very good police force. They knew their stuff. Still, when—*if*— the detective did show up at our house, I could always act super cooperative and tell him I'd prefer to bring Shane to the station and talk there. But instead of going down there, we would escape. We didn't have to take off before he approached us. It must take a while to get a subpoena for Dr. Wilkins's notes, weeks maybe. Court orders and such didn't move nearly as quickly in real life as they did on TV. That meant Morales would hardly show up here tomorrow if he did decide to come, and he could definitely not demand anything of us without a subpoena. Besides, it was likely that he'd find the real killer before the subpoena was ready anyway. If he could even get a subpoena. Maybe it wasn't as easy as I'd assumed.

I chuckled to myself. What had I been thinking? Not only did Shane and I have way more time than I had originally assumed, but we might not have to disappear at all.

Shane cocked his head to the side. "Mom? Are you all right?"

I made myself smile at him. "Yes. Yes, I'm sorry. I was just thinking of something in the book I'm editing. It's very compelling and I'm having a hard time editing that portion."

"Oh. Do you want me to help you?" He grinned at me. "Maybe I can figure it out. It's a thriller, right? I *love* thrillers."

I couldn't help but smile wider. My son was definitely not a full-blown psychopath. What psychopath instinctively offered to help when someone was struggling?

I reached out and caressed his cheek. "No, honey. It's okay. I'll figure it out eventually. Thanks, though. I really appreciate the thought."

I put away the letter I had written in a drawer and got to my feet. "You must be hungry. Let's go make something to eat. Or how about we just order pizza?" Shane loved pizza.

He brightened. "Yay, pizza! Let's order pizza!"

I realized I needed to use the bathroom. "Why don't you call the usual place and order two pizzas? I have to go to the bathroom. You have the number in your phone, right? They should have my credit card on file."

"Yeah. What kind do you want?"

"A small, thin-crust with pepperoni and mushrooms. What else?" I winked at him. I didn't think I had ever ordered another type of pizza but that one from Pizza Hut, our preferred pizza baker. It was my favorite.

"Okay. I'll order it right now."

As Shane started dialing, I made my way out of the study and headed toward the bathroom at the other side of the hallway. I felt like I had made the right decision. It really was extremely unlikely that Detective Morales would come to our house in the next 24 hours and demand we talk to him. He probably would contact us, but it would take a few days at least. Several days.

I entered the bathroom and took my time doing my business. I felt I needed a few minutes alone to decompress. By the time I came out, Shane had moved to the kitchen where he had set the table and was cleaning up the kitchen counter. I had made a salad for lunch and hadn't bothered to clean up after myself a few hours earlier. A wave of warmth rolled through me. My son could be so sweet. He really was a great kid.

"The pizzas should be here in like twenty, Mom," he said as I hobbled into the kitchen and over to the table.

"Thanks, honey. That sounds great." I took a seat and put away the cane behind me.

"Do you want some Pellegrino?" Shane was standing by the fridge.

"Sure, bring me some."

He pulled out a big bottle of the sparkling water and came over to the table where he filled my glass first, then his.

I cocked a brow at him. "You're having Pellegrino? I thought you didn't like it."

"I changed my mind. I'm older and wiser now. It's better for me than soda."

I couldn't help but chuckle a little. "Yeah, that sure is true."

The pizzas arrived when expected and Shane tipped the delivery guy, then returned to the table with the boxes. We devoured our pizzas in silence.

It wasn't until they were almost gone that Shane brought up the subject that would make me lose twelve pounds in the next two weeks. The story that would make me even more convinced that I had to protect my son, do everything in my power to heal him, make him into a functioning adult. After he was done telling me, I couldn't see anything as being his fault.

It was all my fault.

Every single thing he did was because I hadn't protected him from all the evil in the world.

22

"Mom," he said when he had finished eating his pizza and gulped down two glasses of Pellegrino. He wiped his mouth with a paper towel that he had turned into napkins for us. "There's something I need to tell you."

I put down my silverware and focused on him instead of on the remainders of my own pizza. I could instantly tell that he wanted to tell me something of grave importance, so he deserved my full attention.

"Yes, honey. What's going on?"

"I've wanted to tell you for so long." He glanced at some distant spot beside me, as though in a trance. "But I never knew how. It was never the right time. But I'm older now. I feel I can do it now."

Against my will, I was suddenly frowning and there was a painful tugging in my stomach area. Anxiety floated through me. Whatever it was Shane was about to break to me, the one thing I could be certain of was that it would not be anything good. Quite the opposite. I could literally feel it.

He put his big hands before his face, muttering something I couldn't make out. Slowly, he rocked back and forth on the chair. Then he started to cry. In shock, I just stared at him at first.

I put a hand on his shoulder, as upset as he acted. "Shane, honey, what's *wrong?* What's happened? Please don't be afraid to tell me. There's nothing you can't tell me. You know that, right? I'll love you no less no matter what you tell me." *Oh God, please don't have him confess to me that he has murdered someone in cold blood*, I thought, not sure why this was the first thing that occurred to me. I honestly didn't know if I'd be able to keep the promise I had just made him then. I would do my best, but I honestly didn't know how I would react. The mere thought of it made me want to hurl up the pizza on the floor beside me.

He kept crying, his body trembling. He looked so vulnerable, so small and helpless all of a sudden. *No, I will love him no matter what he's done,* I decided. He was my son and he had been traumatized under my watch. Well, mine and Peter's. We were responsible for his behavior, him acting out. *Of course* I would still love him. How could I ever think otherwise?

I squeezed his shoulder with my hand. "Honey, please tell me what's wrong. What happened? You can tell me. I won't be mad, I swear."

At long last, he lowered his hands and showed me his face again. Because of the redness, his teal eyes looked more blue than green, a startling, electrifying blue. I handed him a paper towel for him to dry his wet cheeks with. He took it and dabbed his puffy skin.

"Please don't hate me once I've told you," he whispered.

I grabbed his free hand firmly. "Of course I won't hate you! Nothing you say or do can make me hate you. I love you too much to ever be able to hate you."

He nodded, looking slightly relieved. "It wasn't Uncle Tony who abused me."

I stared at him, the tugging in my stomach increasing in strength, hurting me. I stifled the gasp that wanted to come out of my mouth. I felt dizzy with nausea. I forced myself to get a grip because I was acting ridiculous. Why was I thinking I already knew the answer? I didn't. It could be anyone!

I cleared my throat and held Shane's glance. "Okay. Then who was it?"

Shane's chest rose and fell as he sighed. "It was—it was Dad."

It was too late for me to go to the bathroom and throw up. The pizza was already coming out of me as I turned my head and tried to stand, splattering down on the colorful rag rug on the linoleum kitchen floor.

I leaned as far away as I could from Shane while grabbing hold of the back of my chair and the table edge so I didn't fall over. I continued throwing up until there was nothing left to throw up, merely dry heaves. Cool sweat was suddenly coating my skin under my baggy top. My heart pounded violently in my chest. I felt like I was in a bad dream, but I knew I wasn't.

"Mom," Shane whispered. "I'm so sorry. I didn't mean to upset you that much. I knew you'd be upset. I should've kept my mouth shut. Oh, why didn't I just keep my mouth shut?"

"Please stop apologizing, Shane. It's not your fault. I just wish you'd have told me sooner. A lot sooner." *Or not at all,* a tiny voice inside me whispered. I instantly shut it down.

"I'm sorry."

Wiping my mouth with the back of my hand, I turned to him. "Don't be. I'm glad you told me. Please get me a bucket of hot water, detergent, and some towels. I need to clean this mess up. Okay?"

"Um, sure." He got to his feet and hurried out of the kitchen. I could hear him jog across the hallway to the cupboards next to the bathroom.

"Grab the oldest towels you can find, please," I called out, my eyes watery. I peered down at the big mess I had created, numb inside. Distractedly, I tore off paper towels that I tossed over it. So *Peter* had abused Shane then? His own *father* had abused him? How could I not have known? Suspected? I should have suspected what was going on, but I hadn't. Not even once.

Oh God. Another wave of nausea surged through me, resulting in more dry heaves. They lasted several seconds. What about Tony? What had Tony done to Shane? Nothing at all? Why had he killed himself then? I closed my eyes when the realization rushed through me, and I forced myself to breathe deeply through my mouth. My nose was full of snot. No, that couldn't be. But I knew it could very well be so.

Had Peter killed his own brother and made it appear like suicide? Had he suddenly freaked out that Shane would tell? The more I considered this, the more likely it seemed. Peter could easily have made it look like Tony had hanged himself, then written the confession himself. Tony was already depressed, so no one had questioned the fact that he'd committed suicide.

Especially not after we had read what was in the note that he had left on his pillow in his made bed. After reading that, everyone was thankful and fully understood why he had chosen to finally take his own life. He hadn't been able to look himself in the mirror, for perfectly understandable reasons. He was a monster, and he had known it himself. He didn't deserve to live, and, at the time, I remember thinking that he got away much too easily. He should have been forced to go to jail and have the prisoners rape and torture him to death.

Hanging was much too lenient a punishment for what he had done.

Oh God... So it had been *Peter* all along. Oh God.

The only reason we had known Shane had been sexually

abused at all was because of that suicide note. Why didn't Shane ever tell me? Peter must have scared him into not telling me. It was the only explanation. Seeing what Peter had done to Tony must have really freaked him out. No wonder he had chosen to kill his father. It had been the only way to stop the abuse. Once a pedophile always a pedophile. They always revert back to their old behavior even if they realize they need to stop it.

Another wave of nausea rode through me and I shivered with cold.

God, how Shane must have hated me for letting this happen to him, I mused. I, his mother, who was supposed to make sure nothing bad ever happened to him. Frankly, after learning this, I was amazed that he hadn't tried to kill me, too. I shook my head. His father was a worse monster than I had imagined his brother to be. A full-blown psychopath. Well, as they say, the apple didn't fall far from the tree.

The thoughts speeded through my head as I waited for Shane to return to the kitchen.

Had I ever seen signs of Peter being a psychopath? I searched my mind and couldn't think of a single instance where that suspicion had even entered my mind. He had been a great guy from the get-go. We had met at a beer hall in Astoria, a neighborhood in Queens, when I was twenty-four and he twenty-seven. I, a struggling actress, and he, a junior accountant, at Ernst & Young. The connection between us had been instant and we had started dating seriously right away. We both wanted the same things out of life—a family that we could raise in the suburbs. He would bring home the dough while I pursued my creative urges. First, I'd make it as an actress, then, eventually become a stay-at-home mom. Neither of us had planned on Shane arriving as quickly as he did, but we were nonetheless excited about it even if it meant that I had to ditch my plans to pursue acting. Our son deserved my full attention, especially after we found out the abnormalities in his brain.

Peter had been the perfect man, always happy and attentive. Funny and resourceful. We never ever fought, not even when we found out our son's diagnosis at age three and later, the abuse he'd been through. Mostly, we were insanely, Hallmark-card happy despite our challenges. Maybe that should have raised red flags for me. No one was as good and kind as Peter had been all the time. If anyone was ever grumpy and picked a fight, it was me. Thankfully, Peter had been so adept at putting me in a good mood again that any fight always defused before it could escalate into something serious. My occasional grumpiness was a symptom of me missing the acting a lot the first years as a stay-at-home mom. I simply loved playing different people, submerging myself in their heads, fully becoming them. I had been told I was very good at it, too. Extremely convincing. Peter had cured my agony by suggesting I start to write screenplays. It turned out that it did.

I suppose Peter had been the better actor in the family, I mused bitterly now. He sure had had me and everyone else fooled. I finally understood that he'd been acting all along, to hide what kind of a person he'd really been, the worst of all kinds: a pedophile *and* a psychopath. Yes, he had been an even better actor than me. If he had known just how good he'd been, maybe he'd have pursued such a career himself instead of wasting his talents on accounting.

"Mom?" I turned my head slowly toward the doorway and spotted Shane standing there with a bucket in one hand and a bunch of old towels under his other arm. I forced myself to focus on the here and now. There was nothing I could do about the past.

Together, we cleaned up the mess I had made, no one saying a word in the meantime.

23

We threw out the rag rug instead of attempting to clean it. It was cheap, so it made more sense to buy a new one given its soiled state. We spent thirty minutes scrubbing the blue linoleum kitchen floor with strong detergents that made the sour smell of vomit fade away. The hard, monotonous manual labor was just what I needed in that moment. I didn't want to think about what kind of person I had been married to. I could do that later, when I was alone. Right now, Shane needed my full attention. I couldn't give him that if I was crawling on the floor, bawling and screaming curses at a god I no longer believed existed. Not that I had ever been very religious; I was more of a spiritual person. Now, though, I really didn't think there was a god anywhere, or at least not one I could look up to and love. Making my husband and my son people with psychopathic tendencies, then adding the pedophilia and incest on top of that, was just too much for me to handle that evening.

When we were satisfied it was clean enough, we went to have a seat in the living room, next to each other on the same couch. I felt less sad now and instead anger was flowing through my veins. Ice cold anger and determination to stand by my son no matter what.

He was going to have a good life. I refused to let anything else bad happen to him. With the right treatment, he would evolve into a fine person. Unlike Peter's, Shane's brain was no way near fully developed, so he could definitely be fixed. I was glad that Shane had killed Peter, because, this way, he couldn't hurt anyone else. I didn't even want to think about what other horrors my dead husband might have perpetrated; surely, Shane hadn't been his first victim. Even so, I should focus on what I knew, the damage he had done to our son. Whatever his abuse had resulted in could be reversed if I tried hard enough. Psychology and neuroscience were both young sciences. There was a lot to be discovered yet. I would devote the rest of my life to make sure I found a solution. A cure for Shane. I owed him that.

"Shane," I began and turned my body toward him. "Why didn't you tell me what your father had been doing to you?" I had to know this despite that it would make Shane uncomfortable. I needed to know what else Peter had done to silence our chatty, cheerful son.

He averted his gaze and stared at the black TV screen. He kept picking at his nails.

"Please tell me why," I pleaded with him.

"Dad said he would kill me if I ever told you," he whispered, lowering his gaze to the floor. "I didn't want to die."

Peter had threatened to *kill* him? Even though it only confirmed my earlier suspicions, I felt like I had been shot in the heart in that moment. I couldn't even begin to imagine the trauma Shane had been through. He'd only just turned five when the abuse started. The terror he must have experienced at the hands of a person who was supposed to love and protect him, be his hero, not someone to fear, was incomprehensible. I couldn't imagine the physical pain he must have experienced each time his father violated him. The humiliation. The doctors had explained to both me and Peter exactly what had been done to our son. There had been lots of tearing in the rectal area, so there was no doubt he had been raped. Repeatedly. Oh God.

He turned to look at me then and big tears fell down his cheeks. "I was too scared to tell you. So I killed him instead. I did it on purpose, but I had no choice. Do you think you can forgive me, Mom? I know it's wrong to kill another person. I know you loved him so much, but it hurt so much. I just wanted him to stop."

I pulled him toward me and hugged him close. "Shh," I whispered in his ear. "The one who should beg for forgiveness is me. Forgiveness from you, who's been put through hell on earth. I'm glad you killed him, Shane. I'm just sorry I couldn't have done it for you. He got what he deserved. He was a monster. I can't believe I ever loved a monster." I really couldn't. How could I not have even *suspected* what was going on? It was unforgivable.

I let go of him and placed my hands on his shoulders, holding his gaze.

"Will you ever be able to forgive me, Shane?"

He looked confused. "Forgive you for what? I never thought any of it was your fault. You didn't make him do what he did to me, did you?"

"No, but"—I averted my gaze from my son's—"I should have stopped him before he could hurt you. I should have known. I'm your *mother,* for God's sake! Mothers always sense these kinds of things. Why didn't I?" I realized tears were streaming down my cheeks then, blinding me.

Shane hugged me hard, pressing his cheek to my chest. "Please don't cry, Mom. I'm not mad at you. It wasn't your fault. Any of it. It was his. Only his."

His words only made me feel worse. I hugged him back, stroking his smooth hair over and over. He was such a good kid. Despite everything he'd been through, he was still such an amazingly kind person.

Slowly, we let go of each other. Shane handed me a tissue from a Kleenex box on an end table. Gratefully, I took it from him and dabbed my wet face. He smiled at me.

"Wanna watch a movie?" he asked. "Like, *Star Wars* or *The Goonies?*"

Those two were Shane's favorite movies at the moment. "Or how about *Pretty Woman?* You *love Pretty Woman.* It'll cheer you up."

I ran a knuckle across his cheek. My son was so not a psychopath, trying so hard to make me happy again. "Let's watch *The Goonies*," I said and smiled at him.

24

T he following morning I nearly choked on my morning coffee. I was watching the local news right after Shane had left for school:

"...an anonymous tip to the NYPD has led to a breakthrough in the gruesome murder of Dr. Jonathan Wilkins," the female anchor stated. "The NYPD is now on the lookout for a Caucasian boy about twelve or thirteen years old with light brown hair and piercing blue eyes. He is skinny and around five foot eight. According to the tipster, the boy came out of the walk-up building where Dr. Wilkins lived about three a.m. the Thursday morning when the psychologist was killed. He was wearing jeans and a baggy, light gray hoodie that was stained with blood..."

That was all I needed to hear to pick up my phone and call my son's number.

"Hi, Mom," he answered after the second ring, a little out of breath. "I'm about to walk into the subway. What's up?"

"Come straight back home. Right *now*. Hurry!"

"Why? Is everything okay? Are you okay?"

"I'll explain when you get here. Turn around and hurry home right now. Oh, and one more thing."

"What?"

"Are you still wearing your hat? The Yankees one?"

"Yeah?"

"Pull the visor down as far as you can, so no one can get a good look at your face."

"Um, okay."

"Good. I'll be here waiting for you at home. Hurry!"

I disconnected the call without saying goodbye. If Shane was at the subway station, it would take him about ten minutes to get back home if he jogged. I needed to pack as much of our stuff to bring with us as I could in that time. We had to get the hell out of here, run away somewhere Detective Morales couldn't get a hold of us. He sure as hell would have no problem getting a subpoena for Dr. Wilkins's notes now, and he would probably get it quickly, too. It was perhaps only hours before he came here or to Shane's school and took him into custody. When he found out that Shane had no real alibi—it wasn't like I had actually *seen* my son sleeping in his bed, even if I had no doubt he had—he would have enough probable cause to arrest Shane.

I could not let that happen. I don't know who this kid with the bloody sweater was or what he'd been doing at Dr. Wilkins's building the night of his murder; all I knew was that it couldn't have been my son. Shane didn't kill Dr. Wilkins.

I got the two backpacks that were gathering dust in the walk-in closet and ran around like a maniac, filling them up with essentials for both of us. I was still dependent on the cane to move efficiently, so it didn't go as fast as I wanted it to. I had bought the backpacks last summer so that we could go camping. It turned out that Shane had no interest in such an activity after all, despite having claimed over and over that he had, which had driven me batty. In the end, I had kept the backpacks and now I was glad that I had.

I was almost finished packing by the time Shane walked into the hallway, his cheeks flushed under the hat. He stopped in the doorway, staring at me as I was shoving a couple of his sweaters in one of the backpacks. The other backpack sat on the floor, on the other side of the door.

"What's going on?" he asked. "Are we going somewhere?"

"Yes, you and I will have to take a trip. We might need to stay away from the New York area for a while." I made my way back to his room where I fetched several pairs of socks from a drawer. I had totally forgotten to pack socks, I'd suddenly realized. He hurried after me.

"Why do we have to stay away from the New York area?"

"Because I did something very stupid. I spoke to the detective who's investigating Dr. Wilkins's murder—"

He sucked in a sharp breath. "Is Dr. Wilkins dead? Who killed him?"

"The cops don't know that yet, honey. They only *think* they do, primarily because of me calling that detective and revealing things I shouldn't have. At the moment, you're their best lead, I'm sorry to say. That's why we need to go on a trip. Until things quiet down and they find the real killer."

"I'm their best lead? How can *I* be their best lead? Why would I want to kill Dr. Wilkins? What did you tell the detective? Bad stuff about me? That I killed Dad and took pics of Alice's body?" Shane looked terrified. I couldn't blame him; he should be terrified. Things did not look good for him and it was all my fault. Oh God.

I briefly considered telling him the truth—that I had revealed all my fears to Dr. Wilkins, whose notes would be read by Detective Morales. But that would only serve to upset Shane further, so instead I said, "No, of course not, honey. It's because I was one of Dr. Wilkins's patients and called the cops twice to see how the investigation was going." It was a lame explanation, but it was all I could come up with off the top of my head.

"Why would I be a suspect because of that?"

I cleared my throat and pretended to look for something in the drawer to buy myself time. "Well, I seemed a little too interested in the case. Behavior like that always makes people suspicious. The police will look into my background now, which means they'll end up finding out about you having shot your father. It's in the police reports. Unfortunately, that will be a reason for suspicion. Meaning, the fact that you were involved in the shooting. Mainly, they're grasping for straws because they don't have any other leads. Anything will do at this point, so they'll come after us."

"Okay, but what's the rush?" he asked, crossing his arms over his chest. "Do you think they're on their way to pick me up right *now?*"

I stopped what I was doing and faced him finally. "They reported on the news this morning that the police have received a tip about the killer that matches your description down to a T."

His chin dropped and his lips parted. "They did? Really? That's so weird because I definitely did *not* kill Dr. Wilkins. I swear!" His voice croaked.

I hugged him then. "I know you didn't, but that doesn't matter. It only matters what the police think. This is why we need to get out of the New York area until they find the real killer. We need to leave as soon as possible." I pointed to his backpack. "Check what I've put in it, then add what else you want to bring with you. But only stuff that you'll really need while we're away from home. It could be a while."

"Okay. Can we go stay at the country house? I love it over there."

I clicked my tongue and ruffled his silky, light brown locks. "I know you do, honey, but that's not a good idea. If we go there, they'll find us pretty quickly. It'll be one of the first places they'll come looking for us. Like I said, we might have to stay away a while. Far away. Like in another state far away."

"In another *state*? What about school? Am I not going to school then?"

"Definitely not. We'll have to keep you away from school. If we're lucky and the police arrest someone soon, it won't be for very long. Maybe only a couple of weeks." I smiled at him. "You can afford to miss two weeks of school. You're already ahead in your class."

"Okay. So where are we going then?"

I sighed. "I'm still working on that. Maybe we can go somewhere in the South. Or to somewhere in the Midwest. Like to Iowa. It's really cheap to live there, and no one will think to look for us there. We can take the train to Philly and then take a Greyhound bus farther south or west. Don't worry, I'll figure something out."

"So we might stay in Iowa then?" A frown had appeared on his forehead.

"Yes, honey. I think that would be a good place."

"What about Florida? It's much warmer down there. Like, in Miami. They speak Spanish there and I need to practice my Spanish anyway. You can practice yours while we're there, too. It'll be good for you. You always tell me how you're losing your Spanish."

I couldn't help but smile at him. He was right; my

Spanish was no longer what it used to be, mainly for lack of practice. I'd spent a couple of summers teaching English in Mexico, which was how I had learned to speak Spanish.

"Fine. We can go to Miami instead if you prefer that. It really doesn't matter."

All that mattered was that I could keep Shane away from the police.

25

Before we took an Uber to the train station—I worried there would be cops at the subway stations that might recognize Shane—I made a quick stop at a bank and withdrew 5,000 bucks. I claimed I needed all the cash to purchase a used car. The teller explained that the withdrawal would likely be reported to the authorities and that they might contact me. I told her it was fine. It wasn't like I would be around to answer their questions anyway. (The last part I kept to myself.) Obviously, we would never use one of my credit or debit cards once in Miami or wherever we'd end up, as the cops could track us down that way. We needed to leave as few traces as possible. Neither would we bring our phones or laptops. I was well aware that the authorities could find you when you used your phone, and I was also pretty sure they'd find you if you used your computer. We didn't have time to verify computer use, but it was better to not risk bringing our laptops, which were also heavy. We'd survive without constant computer access while on the lam. There were always public places such as libraries and computer stores we could use to surf the web.

Shane was not happy about having to leave his brand-new MacBook behind. When I told him I'd buy him a new one in Florida, he cheered up a little. Not that I thought I would be able to, but I couldn't think of something better to say right then. He'd get over it.

The $5,000 should last us at least a month if we were careful and only bought absolutely necessary stuff. I purchased the train tickets to Philly with a credit card. I wanted the authorities to see that information and assume we were going in that direction, even staying there. Philadelphia being connected to so many parts of the States, there were too many directions for us to travel in for them to figure out where we had gone anyway.

I had been about to use my credit card to pay for the Greyhound tickets as well. As well connected and afford-able as the Greyhound buses were, they were our best travel option. When it struck me that the authorities would be able to easily determine this purchase as well, I changed my mind and decided that I would use cash instead. I couldn't risk the FBI checking for us at every Greyhound stop. Sadly, it was likely there would be a national manhunt for us now that we'd become fugi-tives. Hopefully, they'd operate for a while under the assumption that we'd remained in the Philly area. Maybe when we reached Miami, we could take the boat over to Cuba. I didn't think the US authorities could do anything to us over there. From what I had been able to gather, the Cuban government wasn't too fond of the United States.

I had decided that I would mail a letter to my parents as well as to the precinct where Detective Morales worked instead of just handing one to my mother that she'd take to him. I couldn't risk my mom forgetting bringing it to him. I'd mark the one for the police station with Morales's name; surely, it would get to him somehow. I would also have my mom call him and tell him we were gone and why. This was by far the best approach. I couldn't have my parents go crazy with worry not knowing why Shane and I were suddenly gone. In the short letter I had written them while in the Uber, I explained that we needed to disappear for a while, and for them not to worry. I had the situation under control. I would eventually get back to them with more information.

I wouldn't get in touch with Shane's school. Surely, the NYPD would contact the school soon enough anyway, looking for Shane.

On the Amtrak to Philly, it had struck me that I would most likely have to show a photo ID in order to travel with the Greyhound. I was pretty sure that Shane wouldn't have to show anything since he was traveling with me and was a minor. I had totally forgotten about this and it was not good. I couldn't have the Greyhound people know we were using their vehicles.

We took the bus over to the Greyhound terminal, which was in Philly's Chinatown. By the time we reached our stop, I had decided that I would pay for tickets down to the northern state line of Georgia. From there, we could use local transportation down to the Florida state line and continue by foot into Florida. We should be able to find a local bus we could get on that would take us farther south in the state. Then we could switch to another local bus and another, inching farther and farther down. It would be a pain in the butt, but I couldn't risk anyone finding out where we were heading. By getting off in the very north of Georgia, it would be hard to figure out where we had gone next.

When I had reached the person in the ticket booth, a tired, thin-haired woman in her fifties perhaps, I told her to give me two tickets for a station in the north of Georgia. She prepared the tickets for me and told me it would be one hundred and fifty dollars.

"I can pay cash, right?" I asked her and reached for my wallet.

"Sure," she replied distractedly.

I found my wallet. "Do you need my photo ID as well?"

She waved her hand no. "That's okay. There are a lot of people behind you I need to get to before my break. Just the payment is fine."

I tried not to stare at her. "Actually, how much would two tickets down to Miami, Florida be? I think we'll go there instead."

She checked her computer screen. "Two hundred and fifty for two."

"Can I have two of those instead?"

"One way?"

"Yes."

Without a word, she prepared the tickets for me. Before she could ask any questions, I pushed the cash she had wanted through the hole in the window. She took it and handed me the tickets. I thanked her and went over to Shane, who was sitting on a metal bench on the other side of the terminal, watching our backpacks. I could hardly believe our luck. Who would have thought it would be that easy to buy the bus tickets? Now I felt silly, having agonized for hours over how we would get down to Miami undiscovered.

"Where are we going?" Shane asked me as I reached him and plopped down beside him, trying not to smile too widely.

"Straight to Miami," I whispered to him. "They never asked to see an ID."

"Yay, that's great!" Shane nearly bounced with excitement. A man in a cheap suit who smoked a cigarette a few feet away turned his head in our direction.

I put a hand on his knee and hissed, "Calm down, honey. We don't want to attract unnecessary attention."

I had already checked the timetable and knew that the next bus to Miami would leave in about two hours. That wasn't a lot of time, but I hoped it would be enough for us to change our looks before we got on the bus. I had already brought a pair of scissors to use for my long, blond hair. All we needed now was dark hair dye to change the color.

"Stay here," I told Shane and walked out of the terminal. I spotted a giant drugstore across the street. With any luck, they should have everything we would need there, including fake glasses and burner phones.

26

Mom was sleeping beside me inside the bus or pretending to be sleeping. I couldn't tell. She was leaning back in the bus seat, her eyes closed while wearing earbuds. She had been listening to music on one of the disposable phones we had gotten back in Philly, but now it seemed she might have passed out. We were driving through the suburbs of some small town in the outskirts of southern Virginia and it was late at night. The moon was high in the dark sky and you could see plenty of stars. I could make out the constellation Orion among them. I took a few pics of it, using my new phone. They didn't come out very good, as the camera quality sucked, but it was better than nothing. I had never before seen Orion, not even at the country house, so it was worth commemorating.

At first I thought it was going to be a lot of fun to go on a trip and skip school for a while, but I was no longer so sure about that. So far, the only exciting thing that I had experienced was spotting Orion. Other than that, I was getting more and more antsy. And bored. Bored as hell. My butt hurt from sitting in the same seat for hours and hours, and the jam-packed bus smelled of B.O., fast food, and stale clothes. Most people in it looked either shady or like they were homeless. Some like they were both. I had already begun to miss my computer and video games. All I'd done the last several hours was stare out the grimy bus window at the landscape swishing by. I'd come to the unexciting conclusion that Pennsylvania and Virginia didn't look much different from New York in the fall. New York state anyway. If we were not near or passing through a city, there were a lot of trees with red and yellow leaves or firs and pines along the highway. Everything was flat and square. A few giant chain stores such as Walmart, Home Depot, and Target popped up here and there. The sky was gray and dreary just like it had been back home most of the time this fall. It rained every now and then. Basically, crap weather all day long. So depressing. I could hardly wait until we would make another stop at some lonely rest area with fast food restaurants. It had only been a couple of hours since we'd stopped at a Burger King where Mom and I had eaten super-sized meals and emptied our bladders. I was already hungry again and wished that I had brought a burger or apple pie or something with me on the bus. Now I'd have to suck it up till the morning. It was one in the morning, so I doubted we'd make another stop until it was time for breakfast much, much later.

Sometimes I passed out in the seat I was so incredibly bored. When I woke up and looked out the window again, I had no idea if the bus had moved one or thirty miles, gone forward or backward. It was all the same out there. I needed to check the time to find out. The last time I checked, I determined that we had about two thirds left of the trip. Ugh.

At one point, I managed to fall asleep and stay asleep till we'd reached our next stop in South Carolina.

Mom woke me up and we headed to an IHOP in the rest area. The sun was crawling up the sky and there were few clouds in sight. Hopefully it would stay that way. The bus driver had informed all of us travelers that we had an hour for breakfast, so Mom and I figured we'd go somewhere other than a burger place this time. There were plenty of those types of restaurants in the area that attracted most of the other people on the bus.

At the pancake place, we got seated at a window table right away. It was pretty empty. Mom wanted me to order from the waiter because she was dead tired and had a headache; unlike me, who'd not only slept but also snored for hours apparently, she had only gotten a few minutes of shuteye. The last thing she wanted to do was talk to people; besides, she thought it could be good practice for me to do it. Make me more comfortable around new people.

Practice for what? I wondered. I had no problem ordering food out at places nor was I uncomfortable around new people. What was she talking about? Not only that, I was the one the cops were looking for, so wasn't it risky for me to talk to strangers when I didn't have to? You would think so, right? Yeah, I had black hair now that made me look like I was a die-hard Marilyn Manson fan, not to mention sick I was so pale, but still. I thought it was pretty obvious that we had both dyed our hair black—Mom's was also much, much shorter after I'd helped chop it off—so why take the risk?

I wanted to ask her that, but I didn't. I had learned a long time ago that Mom had a hard time dealing with criticism of any kind. So I avoided criticizing her as much as possible and agreed to talk to the waiter. Better than getting into an argument. I sighed inwardly and steeled myself when he came over, a guy who didn't look much older than me he was so skinny under the uniform. But he had wrinkles around the eyes and really thin hair, so he had to be.

He smiled at us, displaying a row of stained teeth in which one was missing.

"Howdy, folks, what can I get you this morning?" He looked at Mom attentively, waiting for her to talk to him. But she ignored him and glanced out the window while kicking me under the table. She was obviously not about to let me off the hook.

I cleared my throat.

"Hi," I said, trying not to sound like I was just thirteen, but someone much older. A man. "We would like coffee and two orders of number five."

The waiter jotted down the order on a small scratchpad, then glanced at me again.

"Will that be all?"

I looked at Mom, who muttered something I couldn't hear. I leaned toward her to hear better.

"Tell him to bring a large bottle of sparkling water," she repeated, a little louder, glaring at me through her fake, black-rimmed glasses that made her look even smarter than she was. Uglier too. I was wearing wire-rim glasses myself.

I returned my attention to the waiter, who was checking out some girl outside the window at the moment. A hot girl. I wanted to ask him if he thought he had a chance on her—she was like a nine, but he was only a four, so my guess was she'd blow him off—but I'm not stupid enough to do that. Mom would snap and hit me when we were alone later.

Which, I suppose, I could understand. I could be a pain in the ass sometimes, so I'm not mad about it. She only hits me when I really misbehave according to her, which, fortunately, isn't often. Most of the time she's nice to me. She thinks I'm the shit. I do well in school, but not quite as good as she thinks, though not for lack of trying. I try very, very hard. She loves to tell everyone what a genius I am, when I'm really not. I'm just pretty smart, but I study hard, so I seem smarter. I don't play nearly as many video games as she believes. Most of the time I'm studying like a maniac, because I want her to keep thinking I'm a genius. I want her to be proud of me, love me as much as I love her.

I told the waiter her drink order, and then he left.

Mom grabbed my wrist and squeezed it. "Good job,

Shane! Really good. I told you this trip would be great for you. You'll become a man in the end. You'll see."

I smiled at her, glad that she was pleased with my performance even though I had no idea what she was referring to. But she's been acting weird ever since we left New York, so it kinda fit.

I had the sudden urge for a Coke; I'm not much of a coffee person and my flirtation with sparkling water has ended. "Can I get a Coke?"

"No, honey. Only coffee is included, so you'll have to drink water then. You know we don't have that much cash. I don't know how long it'll take them to find the killer. I don't dare going back with you before they have arrested someone." She was leaning forward and speaking in a low voice.

I wanted to tell her that I actually didn't mind them arresting and interrogating me. I'd be fine, because I'm not guilty of anything. I didn't kill Dr. Wilkins, so why did it matter if I was interrogated? Seriously, I didn't get it. It was like so stupid, but I wasn't about to tell Mom that. I did already in Philly, and she got really mad, telling me she was doing all this for my own good. That I didn't know what was good for me. She doesn't want to see me in jail, she said. I asked her why she thought I would ever end up in jail when I didn't do it. How can they convict me if I'm not guilty? I read about Dr. Wilkins's murder in the paper. He was killed in the middle of the night last Thursday night. I was in bed sleeping then just like every other night. The kid outside Dr. Wilkins's building could have been anyone.

Instead of answering my questions, she just shook her head at me, telling me to be quiet. I was smart, but I didn't understand how the world worked quite yet. For that, I would need more life experience.

I'm thinking this trip will provide a crash course in that.

27

M om and I were in a cheap motel, sharing a grungy room with two uncomfortable twin beds and towels so stiff they could stand by themselves. We didn't have to provide photo ID to stay, which was why Mom picked this place. Also, it was near the Miami Greyhound station. Tomorrow we would find another, more permanent place to sleep.

I was lying on my bed, relaxing with my hands under my head, while she was taking a much-needed shower. It might not be the best bed in the world, but it was way better than the dilapidated, sweaty bus seat. I couldn't tell, but I was pretty sure it had given my butt bruises. I closed my eyes and thought about how we hadn't brought any school material for me to study while we're away. It's not good, especially if we were gone more than two weeks. (Mom keeps telling me she doesn't think the cops will need more than that to find Wilkins's killer, but I'm not so sure.) That means I'll get behind and there won't be much I can do to catch up with the others. There are only so many hours in a day. *Well, I guess Mom will just have to accept then that I'm not the genius she's convinced herself I am,* I thought. I'm lucky if I'll be able to finish the required schoolwork by Christmas break. Forget about getting good grades on it.

Just the thought of her disappointed face when she sees my average grades—or maybe below average—was enough to make me cringe. I hate it when she looks at me like I'm not all that she expected.

Will she hit me?

She's hit me a few times, but it was a while ago since the last time. It first happened after I shot Dad by accident. It really was an accident, but she doesn't seem to believe it. She did tell the cops and everyone else that it was an accident, that Dad forgot to lock the box in the walk-in closet where he kept his handgun. He also forgot to remove the chair he'd taken into the closet to be able to change the lightbulb in the ceiling. That was how I managed to reach the box and get out the gun.

I really thought it was a toy gun, just a little heavier than my other ones. I had no idea it would do what it did when I held it in the bedroom. I was just trying to show it to Dad, who was sleeping on his bed, and I couldn't get a good enough grip around it. It was so heavy and my hands were so small. I had to hold it with both or I would drop it. It went off sometime when I was moving my fingers around it. The loud sound scared me so much I peed my pants and the gun also jumped in my hands like it had suddenly become alive, so I dropped it on the floor.

I didn't understand what had happened to Dad until Mom came running into the bedroom. She started screaming louder than I'd ever heard anyone scream, and then she threw herself on Dad on the bed, covering his body with hers. She cried and wailed his name over and over: "Peter. Oh no, Peter. Oh no. Oh God, Peter. Please don't be dead. Oh God…"

I didn't know how much time had passed before she slipped off him and turned to me. I stood like I was nailed to the floor, unable to move, my pants wet with pee. I'd kept staring at Mom and Dad and I had known something was very, very wrong.

She looked at me like she wanted to throw herself at me and kill me. Her pretty face was dark and furious, her mouth open as she inhaled and exhaled heavily. Her green eyes, flashing with anger, went to the floor beside me where the handgun had remained, a couple of feet away from me.

She'd suddenly lunged at me and slapped my face. It didn't really hurt because I was so surprised. My ear rang and I saw a bunch of tiny stars flitter before me, but that was it.

"You've killed your father, Shane," she hissed at me, grabbing me by the upper arms and shaking me. Tears had begun streaming down my face. "How could you kill your father? Huh?" She shook me so hard my head bobbed. "How could you *kill* your own father?"

As suddenly as she had gotten hold of me, she let go and

ran out of the bedroom. I heard her footsteps fade as she made her way down the stairs, but I didn't move.

I'd remained in the same spot until I heard sirens wailing outside our house. Car doors slammed and people yelled stuff to each other that I couldn't make out. The house shook lightly as the front door opened and people climbed the stairs. Soon, a few men and two women entered the bedroom. A brunette woman in jeans and a white blouse came up to me, sinking down to her haunches and facing me.

"Hi, sweetie, my name is Christina," she said and smiled warmly. She was from somewhere in the South where people speak funny. "What's your name?"

"It's Shane," I could hear Mom say behind me. "His name is Shane. It was an accident. Oh God, it was all a horrible accident. Peter must've forgotten to lock the gun storage..." Her voice sounded like she was crying. She sank down beside me and put two arms around me, burrowing her nose into the crook of my neck. I could feel her warm tears against my skin and it was hard to talk.

"Ma'am," Christina said, her face serious now. Someone pulled at Mom, pulled her away from me. "I need to speak to your son. Please let him go. Please."

Mom was protesting loudly, but more people showed up and it didn't take long until she was gone from me. People were moving around in the room, talking to each other.

Christina returned her attention to me. I was petrified, not sure what was going on. Why were they pulling my mom away from me? I wanted my mom to be with me. What were all these people doing here? Why did my dad remain in the bed? Why didn't he sit up and help me and Mom?

"Shane," Christina said in a soft voice. "I need to ask you a few questions. Would that be okay?"

I didn't know what else to do but nod.

"Okay, good," she continued. "Can you tell me what happened in this room in the last hour?"

"What do you mean?"

She shifted her position. "Why did you go into your parents' bedroom?"

I shrugged. "I don't know. I was bored and I was gonna see what Dad was doing."

"Okay, great. Then what happened?"

I screwed up my face. "Dad was sleeping on the bed. He was snoring, and that means he's sleeping hard. You have to pinch him or he won't wake up then. Then I saw that the closet door was open, so I went in there."

"Okay. You're doing great, Shane. Tell me what happened next."

"I saw a chair in the middle of the closet and I climbed up on it. I've never been that high up in the closet, so I looked around at all the stuff there. That's when I saw the big gray box Mom and Dad have told me I can't ever touch. I was curious about what was inside it. I thought maybe it was candy that they were hiding from me. So I felt the top part and it was loose. I lifted it up and stuck my hand inside. I thought I was gonna feel bags or boxes with candy, but all I felt was a cold, hard metal thing. I pulled it out and saw that it was one of those toy guns I have in my room. I love guns. I've never seen a gun like that. Is Dad gonna be okay?"

Christina blinked a couple of times, then said, "We hope so. Can you please continue the story? You were doing so well. What happened after you found the gun?"

"I stepped down from the chair and took it with me out of the closet. Dad was on the bed and he wasn't snoring any longer, so I was gonna show it to him. Wake him up and pretend I was a cowboy with a big gun. But it was so heavy that I had a hard time holding it. When I finally did have a good grip and pointed it to Dad and was gonna call him, I almost dropped it and then there was this really loud sound and the gun jumped out of my hands. I was confused about what had happened. I just stood there and Mom came running into the room, screaming like she was super mad. She hardly ever screams. She threw herself on Dad and hugged him. Is Dad gonna be okay?"

Christina looked at me for a long, silent moment, then, instead of answering my question, said, "You did great, Shane."

28

Five days had passed since Mom and I left NYC, and the cops have yet to find the person who killed Dr. Wilkins. Can't say I'm surprised. We're enjoying the nice, sunny weather in Miami, and there have been plenty of opportunities for us to practice our Spanish. I may be fluent by the time we return to New York. That would be so cool.

She and I had just finished reading the news on a computer in a public library in downtown Miami. As we both had suspected, there's a national manhunt for us and the FBI is involved. It sure didn't seem like that letter Mom sent Detective Morales has had any positive effect. I'm still the number one suspect. The prime suspect. The authorities showed pics of me and Mom, telling everyone to call a number they're giving out or to email them if they spot us. Thank God we changed our looks so drastically. I really don't look anything at all like those pics any longer with my new black hair and glasses.

Nor does Mom. With her new, stubby black hair and black-framed glasses, I barely recognize her. Apparently, she likes her new look better than I do, because I've caught her staring at herself in mirrors with a pleased smile on her lips. Personally, I think she looks terrible, but I'm not stupid enough to tell her that.

"What about we help them find the killer?" I suggested when we left the library. I turned my face toward the sun and soaked in its rays. The nice weather put me in a good mood and I wanted to do something proactive. Fix this situation. "Wouldn't that be better than just hiding? Seems the cops could use our help."

She tossed me a glance and chuckled. "How on earth would we do that?"

I shrugged my shoulders. "Maybe we could go back up to NYC and see what's up? The authorities must think we're hiding somewhere in the middle of the country for sure, so that would throw them off, right? It's not like they'll think we're so stupid we're going back home, right?"

Mom looked like she was considering what I had just suggested. "It isn't a bad idea actually. Especially if we keep up our new looks. We look so different that people won't recognize us anywhere. Not even in New York. In a few days, I'll be able to ditch my cane, which will help further." She lifted up the brown cane and punched the sidewalk. "I barely need it now, but I've grown fond of it. It's like it's become part of me, almost."

I filled with joy and skipped in place. "So, we're going back then?"

"Not so fast, honey. I need to think it over before we decide what to do. Consider all pros and cons. But today you and I are going to practice meditation."

I stared at her. "Practice meditation? Why do we need to do that?"

She smiled and ran a knuckle against my chin the way she so often did. "Because you need to relax. I do too, but not as much as you do. I've come to the conclusion that meditation is the best way to deal with the stresses of the current situation." She laughed and tossed her head back. "I'm surprised it took me so long to figure it out. I wouldn't be surprised if it's the answer to all our problems." She gave me a conspiratorial wink as though I would know what she was getting at. I had no idea what she was referring to. I decided it was best to just agree with her, though, so I gave a half smile back.

"You'll see, honey," she said and turned her own face toward the sky, soaking in the sun. We had both gotten some color, which made our black hair less jarring. "It's too bad it's not warmer out or we could have meditated outside. In nature. It's a little too chilly still, so our room will have to do. Come on, let's go back home."

We headed back to the old house where we had rented a small studio with a cooking plate and a bathroom where the mirror was broken and most appliances rusty. It had small beds that were so shaky it felt like they'd fall apart any second. I hated it, but I knew we couldn't afford a better place if we wanted the money to last for a while.

Even if we returned home, we wouldn't be able to get

more money from the bank. Of course, maybe we could get it from grandma. She's always kept cash hidden in the house.

We walked through the unkempt garden and around the two-story house to the backside where we had our own entrance, which was something to be happy about at least. The house owner stunk like he hadn't taken a shower in a very long time and looked like he was high on something. His deep-set eyes looked like two piss holes in the snow, a bleary yellow, and his face was full of wiry gray beard.

I hoped I wouldn't have to talk to him again.

Once inside our little place, I threw myself on my small bed. I placed my hands behind my head and watched Mom remove her shoes and jacket. From behind, I would never have recognized her, she looked so different. I made sure my own feet were hanging off the edge of the bed or she would get annoyed that I was making the bed dirty with my sneakers.

She took a seat on her own shaky bed, which was facing mine. A small nightstand sat between them. She crossed her legs so that she sat Indian-style.

"Do you see how I am sitting?" she asked me.

"Yeah?"

"Sit like me. It's a great position for meditation. Remove your shoes before you do it, though. You don't want to get the bedclothes dirty."

Sighing, I pushed myself up into a seated position and leaned forward to remove my shoes. When I straightened, Mom had pulled out her burner phone. She was doing something on it. I crossed my legs and waited for her to look up.

"Okay, this is how we'll do it," she said, meeting my gaze. She put the phone on the bed beside her, then placed her hands on her knees, palms up and the thumbs connecting with the long fingers. "Do you see what I'm doing with my hands?"

"Yes." I did the same with mine.

"This is the ideal position for meditation. Make sure you sit up tall, not slouching."

I made myself taller.

"That looks good, honey," she commented. "Now I'm going to tell you a phrase that you're going to repeat in your mind over and over. For twenty minutes. You cannot allow yourself to think about anything else but this phrase, okay?"

"Um, okay." I honestly didn't think I'd be able to do that. My mind was hyperactive. I was grateful if I could finish one thought before starting on the next. "What's the phrase?"

"'I can never hurt another being in any way. Love is always the answer.'"

Okay, I would *never* be able to repeat cheesy crap like that for twenty minutes. But I would give it a try. It wasn't like Mom would know anyway.

"Got it?" Mom asked.

"Yes." I repeated the words the way I knew she wanted me to do.

"Good boy. I'm going to play some music. As soon as I turn on the music, close your eyes and start repeating the phrases in your mind over and over. Don't stop until the music has finished playing. I know it sounds really boring, but it will do wonders for you. I promise. Ready?"

I nodded and she started the music.

29

"Shane... Shane!" Someone was grabbing my leg and shaking me. I opened my eyes and saw a crazy-looking woman with short, black hair hovering over me. I was confused at first. I had to blink a couple of times before I realized the woman was Mom. What had just happened? Did I fall asleep? We were in our squalid room, the sun filtering in through the window above the nightstand, highlighting a myriad of dust particles floating around in the air.

"Were you able to do it?" she wanted to know, her face eager. "Did you feel like you went into the zone?" She straightened and sat back on her bed.

I pushed myself up into a seated position on my bed, not fully awake yet. At some point during the meditation, I must have fallen asleep. I do remember repeating the two phrases for a while, longer than I had thought possible only to pass out at some point. I guess meditation was not for people like me, who could fall asleep easily.

"I think so," I answered, rubbing my eyes to get the rest of the sleep out of them. "It definitely made me very relaxed." I grinned at her, and she chuckled.

"That's good. Next time, try to stay awake the entire time. You're not supposed to pass out but to reach a higher state. Or zone."

"Did you get into the zone?"

She pursed her lips and narrowed her eyes that were no longer covered by those thick-framed, black glasses; she always removed them when we got to our place. "Maybe a little. It's hard staying so focused. Harder than what one would think. But we'll try again later. Practice makes perfect. Are you hungry?"

"Yeah, starving!"

"Let's go have lunch then."

We pulled ourselves together and left the house. There was a small Cuban restaurant that we had gone to before that we liked, so we went there. Mom told me it would have to be the last time, though, since we needed to save our money. We would need to eat fast food or at home from now on.

We spent the rest of the day walking around the city, sightseeing.

The next few days were spent at the library, at different branches in the Miami-Dade area, where Mom logged onto one of the computers. In the mornings Mom forced me to meditate before breakfast. I can't say I'm getting better at it, but at least I managed to not pass out again. I still had no idea what was so great about it. In addition to staying on top of the news and the investigation, Mom wanted to do some more research in the field of psychology. She was obsessed with psychology, lately more so than ever. I kept asking her why it mattered so much to her, but she refused to give me a straight answer. She told me to play games on my burner phone instead of worrying about what she was up to. Or, better, read a book or two. After all, the library was full of them, so I might as well take advantage of it.

I was bored with the games on my phone already and I was in no mood to read a book, so I found an empty computer and went over there to surf the web myself. If Mom didn't want to look for the killer, I'd do it on my own. At least I was going to try. The problem was, I had no idea where to start. I didn't even know who would want to kill Dr. Wilkins.

Well, I can start by checking out all the news stories that have been written on the subject, I thought. Make sure I had read every single one of them. I had only read the ones Mom had shown me so far, but maybe she had missed some.

An hour later, I was done and none the wiser. In order to have a chance of finding the real killer, we would have to get back to New York City. I highly doubted we'd find him or her down here in Miami. As I waited for Mom to finish her research, I went to the bathroom where I took my time. When I returned to the reading room, I went up to

Mom. She appeared as hypnotized by the computer screen as when I'd left ten minutes earlier.

I went up behind her.

"Finding anything interesting?" I asked her.

She gasped and swiveled her head in my direction.

I chuckled. "Sorry, I didn't mean to scare you!"

She tsk-tsked and shook her head at me. "Well, you did. How are you?"

"I'm good. Just a little bored. We've been here forever." I remained standing next to her chair.

She pushed it out and got to her feet. "Okay, we can leave. I just need to visit the bathroom. Why don't you have a seat and wait for me?" She indicated her chair. "I won't be long."

"Okay," I said and plopped down on the chair. She ruffled my hair and left. I faced the computer and glanced at what she had been looking at. I had expected it to be some article about psychology, but it was a bank statement. I took a closer look at it and saw that it was from her own checking account. A statement of the previous billing cycle, which had just closed.

Why was she checking out her own bank statement? To see how much money we had left? I scrolled down the statement. How much money did we have left? It could be good to know.

I soon found the total and, according to it, we had close to

12,000 bucks. That seemed to be enough for a while. Not that we could access it or anything, or the cops would be able to trace us. She had explained that to me carefully and kept reminding me each time I wanted to buy something we didn't need.

Casually, I went through the stuff she had bought using her card attached to the account. Most of it was food and some stuff from H&M and the drugstore. A few things from Amazon. My mom loved Amazon, the convenience of home delivery. She had used the card to pay a couple of bills, one for our cell phones and another for the electricity.

I was about to pull up another site to check the weather for tomorrow when something in the statement caught my eye. She had paid a cab twice on the same day. Mom never took cabs, claiming they were an unnecessary expense. Why had she taken cabs that day? One ride came to almost twenty-three bucks and the other to twenty-five. That was a lot of money. I had to ask her about it. I looked closer at the charge, clicking the first one open. It said the taxi ride had taken place the day before the charge had gone through. I clicked on the second cab charge. It said the same thing there.

I changed my mind about asking her about the cab rides when I realized they had occurred the same day that Dr. Wilkins was murdered.

30

"Is everything okay?" Mom asked, standing behind me suddenly. Mere seconds had passed since I had discovered the weird cab charges. Quickly, I moved the screen up to the same place where it had been when she had gone to the restroom, hoping she wouldn't notice what I had been staring at. "You look worried."

I gave a casual shrug. "I'm not worried. Why would I be worried?"

"I don't know." She peered at me for a moment, as though sizing me up, then smiled and adjusted her thick-framed glasses. "Are you ready to leave?"

"Yeah," I said and pushed out the chair. "Want me to log out?" I indicated the computer screen with her bank information displayed.

"Yes, please."

I closed the browser and then we walked out of the

library. The sun had disappeared behind a few large, dark clouds and it felt chillier outside, matching my new mood. It didn't take long before I could feel sticks of rain on my skin. Mom was talking about something she had read in an article about the benefits of meditation. I was barely listening, my mind going a mile a minute, trying to figure out why she had taken such expensive cab rides the day Dr. Wilkins was murdered. Where had Dr. Wilkins lived? That tidbit of information had been mentioned several times in the news articles about his murder. I searched my mind and soon remembered what it had said. Dr. Wilkins had lived in the seventies between Third and Lexington Avenue on Manhattan, a neighborhood known as the Upper East Side. We lived smack in the middle of Queens, so a cab to the Upper East Side would cost somewhere between twenty and twenty-five bucks, tips included. I knew this because I had recently ridden a cab back home with a friend after we had gone to see a play in the Upper East Side area. My friend's mother had insisted we take a cab home, so we had. She had given my friend money to pay with and I remember how we had discussed how much tip one should leave on a twenty-one-dollar fare.

I scowled lightly. What did it matter where Dr. Wilkins lived? Did I actually think Mom had used her card to pay for cabs so she could travel comfortably to Dr. Wilkins's house and kill him? That was ridiculous! Why would she do such a thing?

But then why had she used cabs twice that day? She never ever took cabs.

I could always ask her, but for some reason I didn't want to do that.

"Are you listening to me, honey?" she asked as we walked down a street with queer storefronts on one side. It had stopped raining, thank God.

"Yeah, sorry. I was just thinking about something I saw online." I made myself smile at her.

She grabbed my arm hard and stopped in her tracks. "What did you see online?"

Her face had gone dark and she was staring at me. What was wrong with her? Why was she squeezing my arm like that? I instantly stopped smiling.

"Ouch, that hurts," I whimpered and tried to shake myself loose. Mom only grabbed onto me harder. She had hurt me before when I misbehaved, but I couldn't remember the last time. It had been a while. I couldn't see what I had done wrong now, either.

"What did you see online?" she repeated, narrowing her eyes.

"I'll tell you if you let go of my arm," I muttered, annoyed.

Thankfully, she did and said in a much kinder tone, "Sorry about that. I have PMS today. Please forgive me, honey. I didn't mean to hurt you. What did you see?"

"Just that the person who killed Dr. Wilkins used a large knife from Crate & Barrel. The same kind we have. The kind with the weird, bubbly blade." I regretted saying those words as soon as they had leaped off my tongue.

Where had they come from? I didn't know what kind of knife had been used to kill Dr. Wilkins, did I? There hadn't been any mentions on what kind of knife had been used, only that it had been a kind of knife sold at that store.

Mom gazed at me with a funny expression for which I couldn't say I blamed her.

"You're saying you saw the murder weapon mentioned in one of the articles you read about his murder?" she asked after several seconds passed.

"Um, yeah," I lied. It was in that moment that I realized why those words had come to me in the first place. We had been missing our own Crate & Barrel knife for a while. It was my favorite knife to cut stuff with because it was so sharp and, lately, I couldn't find it anywhere. I used it for everything. When I asked Mom a while ago if she had seen it, she'd said no.

"Oh," was all she said to that, much to my relief. I really wasn't in the mood to go into detail about the knife.

She kept talking about the benefits of meditation all the way to the grocery store and this time I made sure I paid attention. We bought more sparkling water, crackers and cheese, and fruit for our house. A jumbo bag of sour patches. When we were back to our studio, Mom stopped and turned to face me just as we were about to enter the place.

"I think your suggestion is a good one," she said to me.

"What suggestion?" I had suggested a whole bunch of

things in the store, one of them being that we should have burgers and fries for dinner at the local McDonalds. Mom said she would think about it. I hoped she was referring to eating burgers tonight.

"That we should go back to New York and track down the killer on our own. It really does seem like the cops have no idea what they're doing or they would have come up with some suspects by now. It's been more than three weeks since Dr. Wilkins was killed."

"Really?" I could hardly believe my ears. So we were going back then? Great! I was beginning to get sick of Miami, and especially the studio apartment we were sharing. And all we did was hang at the different libraries. It was good use of our time, according to her, since we needed to be frugal. It was too cold to swim in the ocean, another cheap pastime, so unfortunately that was out. Mom didn't want me to get too friendly with other kids here anyway, so she was happy I was mostly with her. My burner phone had the worst camera, so I couldn't even go out on excursions and take pics to pass the time. I missed my friends back in New York a lot more than I had thought. I even missed going to school. I hated my ugly black hair, so I did my best to avoid mirrors.

Thank God Mom had come to her senses. I suddenly couldn't stop smiling.

"When are we going?" I asked her as she opened the door to our mini-apartment with the key we shared.

"Hang on," she said and pushed the door open. "Let's talk more about it when we're inside."

I followed her into our little home, never before having been so eager to do so. She took a seat on one of the chairs next to the rickety kitchen table and faced me again.

"I was thinking we'd leave tomorrow," she said. "How does that sound?"

I grinned big at her. "Awesome!"

She returned my grin and ruffled my hair. "Then that's what we'll do."

31

Getting back to New York was even more painful and tedious than it had been going to Florida, primarily because the ticket salesperson in Miami refused to sell Mom tickets without her showing her photo ID. So we had to take local buses, stopping in various cities throughout the Sunshine State until we found a ticket person who didn't care about ID's. Unlike me, Mom was in no rush to get back, so I didn't complain. I was worried that she'd change her mind if I did. Or get mad and stare at me with those freaky eyes. She could act so weird at times, snap for no reason or stare at me like she wanted to kill me. For as long as I could remember, she had been doing that, some years more than others. She claims it has to do with her monthly cycles when I mention it. Don't they have meds for that? I heard somewhere they did. Mom should take them because she's freaking me out. Not that I would ever tell her that.

She was really freaking me out in the months after I had

shot Dad. She cried nonstop every day, sometimes down-right wailing, like she was hurting so bad she couldn't control herself. I was crying too, but more because she was so upset, not because I was. I had hated Dad for what he did to me and didn't regret having shot him, even if it had actually been an accident. I had just pretended to kill him, because, deep inside, I had wanted to, but I could never do such a thing on purpose. I had had no idea the gun I was holding in my small hands had been a real one. I swear.

That wasn't what Mom thought—I know she thought I did it on purpose no matter what she claims. She has always thought so, from the day it happened even though she told the cops it was all just a terrible accident. Over the years, she sometimes opened the door to my bedroom and peered at me with a mixture of hate and anger in her eyes, the same kind that she had when she had yelled at me after I shot Dad. Like she had wanted to kill me. That look remains etched in my brain. She thought I was sleeping those nights, but I had always awoken, the burning feel of her hot gaze on me rousing me. I had squinted at her through my long eyelashes, barely opening my eyes. When she'd left a minute or so later, I had fallen back asleep and, in the mornings, I hadn't been sure if it had all been a dream or not. If I hadn't caught her doing it the other night, I would still have thought those occasions had only been dreams. This latest night, which took place the last night we slept in that squalid place I loathed so much, she had been lying in her bed on the side, facing me, and so had I.

Like those other times, I had suddenly awoken from the

distinct feeling that someone was glaring at me. She had been glaring at me that night, just like she had glared at me over the years. The difference here had been that I had looked straight into her eyes for several seconds, and there was no question she had noticed me. Her hands tucked under her cheek, she had stared at me with hate and anger, just like I remember her having done so many times before. It had freaked me out to the point that I had opened my mouth to ask her why she was looking at me like that, but before I got a chance to do that, she had closed her eyes and flipped her body over, so she had ended up facing the wall instead.

I had remained in the same position until I eventually fell asleep again, stiff with anxiety. Had she just been sleeping and opened her eyes? I was pretty sure sleep-walkers kept their eyes open, which was why people thought they were really awake when they weren't. I thought about it some more and decided that this must be what had happened—she had opened her eyes while still asleep. I conveniently forgot about the times she had looked at me with the exact same expression a couple of times when I had returned home from a friend's house and she had been on the couch in the living room, watching TV. Not saying a word, she had just glared at me when I'd been about to walk up to the couch. Glared at me like she wanted to do me harm. She hadn't even returned my greeting hello.

Those times I had asked her if she was okay and that look on her face had instantly disappeared and been replaced with a soft smile. She had run a hand over her face and apologized, either blaming PMS or claiming to have been in her own world.

I know I've been sexually abused by my dad, but I can hardly remember any of it, for which I'm very glad. The few pieces I do remember make me all cold and nauseous. Him touching me down there. Him wanting me to touch him down there. Him sticking things inside me that hurt. Him forcing me to take his pipi in my mouth and me nearly choking.

But even though he did all these horrible things to me, I still loved him when he didn't do them. It was very strange, but I did. I didn't want him to die. Except for on those nights he came to see me to play with me like he called it, he was a fun, nice dad. I just wanted him to stop hurt me and make me do those things to him. I was happy when it all stopped, though, and I'm ashamed when I think about that.

It was because I loved him and because I knew Mom loved him so much that I didn't tell anyone the truth, that it had been Dad who'd molested me, not Uncle Tony. I didn't want Mom to get upset. She was already so upset he was dead.

Now that I think about it, the only reason I told her the truth the other week was because she had looked at me in that strange, evil way when I had been about to enter the living room recently. And she had done it for so long that it had really creeped me out. So I decided that I would tell her the truth at last. When I turned 13. It seemed she secretly hated me for having shot Dad. I had suddenly felt convinced that this was so, and I didn't want her to hate me. I wanted her to love me as much as she said she did.

We had finally gotten to Philly from where we'd take another Greyhound back to NYC. It took us almost three days instead of barely two like when we went in the other direction. The NYPD had yet to find a suspect for Wilkins's murder, so Mom and I both felt we needed to help them out. I'm seriously beginning to wonder just how good a police force they are. I mean, how hard could it be to find the killer? It had to have been one of his patients, maybe the son of one of them, the guy that had been outside Dr. Wilkins's apartment building. As soon as I found out who Dr. Wilkins's patients had been, I'd work that angle. We were not worried about hanging around the New York area, because we both really did look different. And I was more often than not wearing an oversized hoodie that shielded my face anyway. On the days I didn't, I would wear a ball cap to hide my face. People wouldn't be able to recognize us. It was not like anyone expected us to be there anyway. The police had made that clear in the news; we were suspected to be hiding out somewhere in the country and the FBI was looking for us.

We went to a small pub where we'd be having a late lunch before taking the bus, which would depart in an hour and a half. I ordered a mountain of fries and a burger, as well as a chocolate shake from the bartender. Mom, much to my surprise, ordered the same.

We were seated at the corner of the long bar so we could get a good view of the TV mounted on the other side of the bar counter, in the middle of all the rows of hard liquor. We asked the bartender if he could put on CNN, which he did. It was almost two in the afternoon and we were hoping for updates about the investigation.

We didn't worry the bartender would realize who we were. The pics of us displayed on TV looked nothing like the way we did now.

We had only been watching CNN for ten minutes when there was breaking news: a teenager had been arrested in connection with the Wilkins murder.

32

Mom and I both stared at the screen, taking in the news, which only lasted for about twenty seconds. Then we turned to look at each other.

"Did you catch all that?" she asked me in a discreet tone. We didn't want to attract the attention of the bartender or other patrons of which there weren't very many, fortunately. The bartender was in the middle of talking to a man at the other end of the bar, and it seemed neither of them had noticed what the anchor had just reported on TV. "It all went so fast I could barely keep up."

"Yes, I think so," I said. "They've arrested a teenager for the Wilkins murder."

Mom's already wide eyes got wider behind the square glasses. "That's what I thought was said. Well, that's just *great*, huh?" She squeezed my knee and smiled big at me. She leaned close. "Didn't I *tell* you it would all work out?"

"Yep," I agreed and returned her smile. "Does that mean I can stop trying to hide my face all the time and change my hair back to normal? I'm seriously tired of looking like an emo boy. It's so not my style. And these glasses are so friggin' uncomfortable." I adjusted the fake glasses so they squeezed my nose less.

She smiled and ran a knuckle along my jawline. "Soon, honey. Soon. Let's get back to the city first. We want to be a hundred percent sure it's the right guy. We need more information about him and the arrest before we can let down our guard. For all we know, they made a mistake and will let him go."

I frowned at her. "Why would they arrest him if they're not sure he did it?"

Mom shrugged. "Everyone makes mistakes, honey, even the police. Not that I think that's what's happened here, but it's better to be safe than sorry. We need to hear about the specific reasons he was arrested to have a better idea. It'll take a while before that's reported, like a day or two, I'm guessing. When we know that and can feel reasonably certain he's the real deal, we can go back to our regular lives. Are you done eating?"

I pushed the plate away. "Yeah. I'm stuffed."

"Good." She checked her watch. "We have forty-five minutes to kill before the bus leaves. How about we go do some meditation on the benches outside? It's nice and sunny, so it should be okay to sit there if we keep our coats on."

"Okay," I said, even though I wasn't in the mood to meditate at all. It was so boring, but Mom insisted, so I knew I'd better just agree. She kept telling me how crucial it was for my brain to meditate every single day, and how I would be so grateful when I was older that she'd made me do it.

I had my doubts about that.

She paid the check and we headed outside. Once we reached the benches, we plopped down on the only empty one. She turned to me.

"Are you ready?"

I merely shrugged in response and placed my hands on my knees before she could tell me to do it. Hers were already on her knees.

"We don't need music to do it here," she said. "Just focus on your mantras. Say them over and over and over. Really, you shouldn't have to have any music when meditating. It's just for beginners to help them get in the right mood."

I wanted to tell her that I was definitely a beginner still, having meditated only a few times, but it was best to keep my mouth shut.

She suddenly scrunched up her face.

"What?" I asked.

"I need to go to the bathroom," she replied. "I should go before we start. Wait for me here and don't start until I'm back." She got to her feet and pushed down her tote bag from the bench in the process. Lots of stuff fell out from it on the old asphalted road.

"Crap," she muttered. She bent over and began gathering the keys, the wallet, the gloves, the chap stick and stuffed it back into the bag. I had bent over as well and helped her gather the stuff. I got hold of a couple of hairbands, chewing gum, and a small hourglass that I had never seen before. It was very pretty, so I took a moment to look at it.

"Wow, this is so cool," I exclaimed, as if hypnotized by the hourglass. "Where did you get it?"

"Toss all of it in here," Mom said by way of answering, holding her tote bag open. I wanted to keep looking at the fascinating hourglass, but her expression dared me to contradict her, so I tossed it back inside.

She dropped the bag on the bench beside her and told me not to let it out of my sight.

"I won't be a minute," she said and hurried toward the pub, which was near the row of benches.

"Okay," I said and glanced in the direction of where a bunch of girls were standing around, talking to each other. As soon as Mom had disappeared into the pub, my eyes went to her tote bag on the bench. Before giving it a second thought, I had stuck my hand inside it and pulled it open. I wanted to take another look at that cool hourglass.

I found it almost right away and took it out. It was made of wood and gold metal and smooth glass. The sand inside was of different colors and glittered in the sunlight. I realized that it was the way the sand glittered that made it so sparkling and mysterious-looking.

I had never before seen it. Mom must have picked it up somewhere during our trip. Where had she gotten it and why hadn't she shown it to me? She knew I adored stuff like that. Weird.

As I put it back in the tote, my fingers bumped into something square, thin, and firm in a side pocket. Frowning, I pulled it out to see what it was. It was a letter that was scuffed around the edges. There was a stamp on it. I checked the address. Who was it for?

Attn: Detective Ivan Morales

19th *Precinct*

153 East 67th Street

NY, NY 10065

The wrinkle between my brows deepened. What was this? It couldn't be the letter Mom was supposed to have mailed to that NYPD detective, could it? Had she forgotten to mail it? It sure looked like that. Well, now it was too late since they had already arrested someone. I had to ask her about that when she got back. I was dying to see what she had written him. She had been so secretive about it when I'd wanted to know what was in it. I just knew it was a bunch of stuff that would make him focus on other people, not me.

"Honey?" I heard Mom's voice call me from afar. I turned

my head in the direction of the voice. She was standing next to a small white truck outside the pub.

"Yeah?" I called back.

"Do you want ice cream? They're selling ice cream here."

I smiled at her. I loved ice cream. "Yeah definitely!"

"Bring my bag and we'll buy some then."

I grabbed her tote bag and was about to put the letter back where I'd found it when it struck me that I might as well keep it. I was dying to know exactly what she had written the detective. If she had forgotten to mail it, she wouldn't realize that I had taken it anyway. I could always mail it after I had read the letter if it turned out the cops had arrested the wrong person.

Sticking the letter into my hoodie pocket, I hurried over to where she was standing, shading her eyes against the bright sun.

33

We arrived at the Port Authority Bus Terminal at seven o'clock that same evening. This final trip had gone in a flash, very smoothly, but I was still excited that we were done with buses for a while. My butt could use a break.

A few minutes later, we were walking along 42nd Street toward Times Square, bumping into the masses of people that were always walking around there. The sun had set an hour ago, so it was pretty dark out, enhancing our disguises.

"Are we going home now?" I asked Mom when we were near the subway station.

She glanced at me like I was crazy. "No, honey, what if the cops are still there? Waiting for us to return. We can't go there!"

I frowned at her. "Why would they be there when they've already arrested the guy who did it?"

She rolled her eyes at me. "I already told you that we can't just count on him being the killer. It might be a way for them to trick us and get us to come back, thinking just what you're thinking. At the very least, we'll need to wait a few days before we go home. You know, see what they have to say on the news regarding this guy. If it does look like he's the killer, we'll go home."

"Okay, so where are we going to sleep tonight then?"

"At a hotel I know where you can pay cash. You don't have to give your name or anything else, so no one will know it's us."

"Oh. That sounds like a shady hotel."

She laughed. "It is a *very* shady hotel. Normally, I would never bring you there, but we really don't have much choice if we want to stay incognito. Hopefully, it won't be for long."

"Okay. How are we getting there?"

"We're walking. It's not that far. Only a couple of miles. We shouldn't waste money on a cab or even the subway when it's so close. Do you think you'll be okay carrying the backpack that far?"

I scowled at her. "Of course I'll be okay. What do you think I am? A kid?"

She laughed again and ruffled my hair. "No, how could I ever think that? You're my little superhero. A man. Nothing's too heavy for you."

"Exactly," I grunted.

"Then let's go there. It shouldn't take us more than thirty minutes."

By the time we had reached the neighborhood where this shady place was supposed to be, I was exhausted. Not that I was about to admit that to Mom, though, who herself looked beat. I had never before been in such a decrepit-looking area. The old asphalt was full of potholes and the trashcans were overflowing. A couple of buildings were boarded up. The few people who walked on the street were poorly dressed and moved like they had the whole world on their shoulders. Their faces were blank and no one made eye contact. There was a sour smell mixed with pot in the air. If the shady hotel was in this area, I could totally see why the people who lived there didn't care either way. It didn't look like they cared about themselves either.

A businessman-type in a nice suit and a woman with lots of makeup, big bleached hair, and tall black boots came out of the five-story building Mom claimed was the "hotel." I quickly realized it was more of a brothel. A whorehouse. The woman was holding onto the man's arm and giggling in his ear as we walked by them.

"That was a pro, right? Who was—" I asked Mom and turned my head to keep looking at the couple. I didn't get a chance to finish my last question.

"Stop staring, Shane," Mom snapped and pulled my arm. "And, yes, probably," she added as we entered the building with its dimly lit hallway and dull carpets that had seen better times. A set of old wicker seats with a table in the middle sat in a corner. Facing the wicker set was a small ticket booth covered by glass and that was built into the wall. I could tell that someone sat in that booth, which looked very illicit.

Mom strode up to the woman in the booth, who looked to be severely overweight and had charcoal hair with silver streaks in it. She had lots of hot pink lipstick clearly applied in an attempt to make her thin lips look fuller. They so didn't. I stood closely behind Mom, who smiled and leaned toward the woman.

"Hello, can we get a room for a night or maybe two?" she asked.

The woman looked her up and down, then her gaze moved to me and she cocked a painted brow as if mildly surprised. But she didn't say anything, just grabbed a key from the wall beside her and told Mom that the cost was 50 bucks a night.

"And you have to pay before each night to get the room," the woman stated in a husky voice.

"Okay, we'll pay you for this night now, and then in the morning, if we decide to stay another, we'll pay the rest. Is that okay?" Mom pulled out fifty bucks in ten-dollar bills from her wallet.

"Yes," the woman replied and placed the key on the small shelf attached to the booth. She reached for the cash through the narrow hole under the glass and pushed the key to Mom. She had the longest, pointiest nails I had ever seen and they were painted in some scary dark color. As they were hashing out the details, I was still struggling to believe that Mom wanted us to stay in this seedy place —it was so not her style—but I figured she knew what she was doing and that we were desperate. It would only be for a day, max two, and I could survive that.

When a cleaning lady came around a corner, pushing a cart full of supplies, I felt a little better. If they had a cleaning lady, it couldn't be too bad, I told myself.

Mom grabbed a hold of my arm and told me to head for the steep stairs. We were going to the second floor. We mounted the long stairs in silence and continued into one out of four doors on that floor. The door had been left ajar and it smelled surprisingly okay inside the small studio-like space.

There was only one big bed there, queen-size, a chair and a table, a cooking plate above a small refrigerator in a corner and what looked like a bathroom attached to the room. An old TV sat on a small dresser facing the bed.

Mom removed her backpack, which was bigger than mine, and plopped down on the bed.

She placed her hands behind her head and leaned back, gazing at me. "I know it's not a luxury place, but it's clean, that I can promise you. We won't get bedbugs from sleeping in this bed."

"Good to know." I removed my own backpack and dropped it on the floor. "I need to use the bathroom."

I crossed the small space over to the bathroom and

walked inside, closing the door. It was old and rusty and the toilet bowl was stained, but it did smell like stuff was clean at least. I did my business and hurried back out.

Mom was lying on the bed, looking like she was sleeping. I curled up next to her and closed my eyes, too. It didn't take long before I had fallen into a deep slumber.

34

When I woke up, it was dark outside the window. I could spot the outline of a moon, which was half full, behind a few flimsy clouds in the night sky. There was a medium-sized window right above the bed with thin curtains that had been left open. At first I was confused as to where I was, but then I saw Mom lying beside me on the still made bed. *Wow, we must have slept for a while, both of us more tired than we had thought, passing out like that,* I mused. I wondered what time it was.

I pushed myself up into a sitting position, careful not to wake Mom. The bed felt sturdy, not like it was about to collapse like the ones down in Miami. I was still wearing my jeans and oversized hoodie. Placing my feet on the carpeted floor, I padded over to where I had hung my jacket on the hook attached to the door and found my burner phone. I checked the time on it. It was about four thirty in the morning.

Turning around, I glanced over at Mom. She appeared to be sleeping soundly, breathing deeply. She always complained about what a poor sleeper she was, so I was happy to see that she for once had managed to get to sleep and then stay asleep. I myself felt wide awake and didn't feel like crawling back into bed. And I was hungry. I was pretty sure that I had spotted a bodega as Mom and I had made our way over to this shady place. Like a block or two away. I should head over there and see if it was open. Sometimes those places were open 24/7. If not, there had to be a 24-hour drugstore somewhere close.

I could get some cash from Mom's wallet and buy stuff to eat and soda to drink. The thought of salty potato chips and peanut M&M's made my mouth water. But was it safe to walk around in this neighborhood all alone at this hour? It didn't seem like it.

I decided that getting my hands on some goodies to eat and drink was more important than my safety. Besides, on second thought, I doubted it was a dangerous area. Yes, it had a whorehouse and was totally rundown, but that didn't mean it was dangerous to be here.

I found Mom's wallet in her tote bag and dug out a twenty-dollar bill that I would use. Then put on my shoes and jacket and snuck out of the room.

Thankfully, it wasn't dark in the hallway, so I could easily find my way to the stairs. I walked as quietly as I could down to the entrance lobby, not sure what to expect. With the exception of someone seated inside the glass-covered booth in the wall, the area was empty and dead quiet. As I passed the hole, I noticed the person inside it. It was a different one now, a much younger and prettier woman. She looked up and smiled at me.

"Can I help you?" she asked.

"No, I'm just going out for a walk. I can't sleep. My mom and I are staying in 2 D. She's still there. I'll be back soon."

"Oh, okay," the girl said and returned her attention to something in her hands, maybe a book or a magazine, I couldn't tell.

I didn't meet anyone else on my way out of the building, nor did I spot anyone on the street that I walked on. While it was dark out, there were enough working street-lights in the area to see okay. It was easier to remember my way around than I had expected, and it didn't take very long before I spotted the convenience store we had passed earlier. It was lit, so it appeared it was one of those that were open 24/7.

Yes, I thought, excited. It was chilly and damp outside, and I was not in the mood to walk around more than a few minutes. Plus, my stomach was rumbling with hunger. I could hardly wait until I could stuff myself full with chips and M&M's, maybe some sour patches, wash it down with lots of soda. I hurried up to the store and pushed open the heavy door. Except for the short, Hispanic-looking guy behind the counter, there wasn't a soul in the place. He glanced up at me from the phone in his hand and gave me a bored look, then ignored me.

I took my time scouring the shelves for the right potato chips, chocolate, and candy. I decided that I would only get chips and M&M's, a king-size bag. Then I went over to the fridge and tried to make up my mind whether I wanted Coke or Pepsi. I was deeply torn. I preferred Coke, not Diet Coke, but all they had was Diet Coke and real Pepsi.

I turned around and sent the guy behind the counter a look. He didn't react, so I called out: "Excuse me, but do you have real Coke?"

"Nope. We're sold out. Whatever is in the fridge is all we have." He said all that without looking up from his phone once.

I sighed to myself. Fine, I'd have to do with the Pepsi then. I couldn't stand anything diet; it tasted so fake. I opened the fridge and got a large Pepsi bottle, then headed over to the counter to pay.

Twenty minutes later, I was back at the whorehouse where I took a seat on one of the old wicker chairs in the lobby. I didn't want to wake Mom with my chewing and drinking. She wouldn't be too happy when she saw how much candy and stuff I had bought anyway. If you asked her, I was eating way too much crap. Well, she did too, but she conveniently forgot about that.

As I devoured the potato chips, I paged through a *New York Post* from a few days ago that someone had dropped on the unsteady glass wicker table. Buried in the middle, there was a story about Dr. Wilkins's murder and the investigation, and how the authorities were still on the lookout for us, whom they believed were hiding somewhere in the country.

I remembered then that I had the letter Mom was supposed to have mailed to Detective Morales in my hoodie pocket. I should open it and see what she had written him.

I placed the large soda bottle and the bag of chips I had systematically been emptying on the table, then got the letter from my pocket. I considered briefly whether I should try to open it in the flap, so that I'd be able to seal it again when I was done. I checked the flap, which was tightly sealed. *Hmm.* It would be hard to do without it looking like the letter had been tampered with. It suddenly dawned on me that I could just get a new envelope and copy the address if I sent it later. Mom would never know I had taken it, and neither would Detective Morales. He didn't know what her handwriting looked like.

I ripped open the envelope and pulled out the folded sheet of paper inside.

Unfolding it, I got ready for an interesting read.

But there was nothing to read. The sheet was completely blank.

I stared at the blank sheet, wondering if something had happened to the words. As I took a closer look, it sure didn't seem like it. The sheet was completely untouched.

I chuckled to myself. *Yeah, well, moron. Of course they didn't just disappear. Where would they have gone?* I checked the envelope to see if maybe I had missed additional sheets inside it. But it was completely empty. All that had been in that envelope was this blank sheet of paper.

I scratched my head. Why had Mom put a blank sheet of paper in the envelope? Was it possible that she had made a mistake? That must have been what had happened. *I guess it doesn't matter if I mail it now,* I thought. I put the sheet back in the envelope and the envelope in my pocket. I made a mental note of asking Mom about it later. Informing her that Detective Morales hadn't gotten the letter she had wanted to send him.

I read through the article in the paper a little more carefully to see if I could learn something new, or if it was different from the ones we'd read online.

The only thing I learned wasn't something I didn't already know. It was just something I had forgotten, that Dr. Wilkins's first name had been Jonathan. Not that it was all that important.

I put the paper aside and finished eating the chips, then walked back up to our room. I could eat the M&M's there without risking waking Mom. Unlike the chips, eating M&M's didn't make as much noise, I told myself. Not if I chewed lightly at least.

35

Mom was no longer in the bed when I walked into the room. The bathroom door was closed and it sounded like the shower was running. The light in the ceiling was on, softly illuminating the bed and everything else around. I wondered if that was on purpose or if it was just a coincidence due to a soon-to-be-expired lightbulb. There was no lampshade around the bulb, so I figured it was the latter. They didn't seem to care about sprucing up things around here more than absolutely necessary. I realized for the first time that there was a security camera attached to a corner in the ceiling. An old-looking camera, but still. That was more than I had expected of this place. I guessed they wanted to be sure nothing too freaky happened here. I wondered what the people using the rooms thought about it.

Mom's tote bag was lying sideways on the bed, her wallet, a pack of Tampax, a keychain, and that pretty hourglass with the glittering, multi-colored sand next to it.

I stared at the hourglass for a moment, then walked up to it. There was something weird at the bottom of it. What was that rust-like dark color? I picked it up and took a closer look at the stains on the light wood and frowned. Wait, was that blood? Old, dried blood. Or was it actually rust? I couldn't tell. I smelled the stains and I thought they did have a faint smell of blood to them. Suddenly, I was no longer feeling like eating any of the M&M's I had brought up, even though I hadn't even opened the bag yet and I loved M&M's. Instead, a quiet sense of nausea spread inside me, and my chest felt uncomfortably tight. In addition to the creepy stains, I had just discovered that there were two letters carved into the bottom of the hourglass.

J W, it said in swirling font.

Not wanting to look at the letters and the blood any more, I flipped the hourglass around. Watching the glittery sand slip through the narrow hole connecting the top with the bottom was so soothing, and right then I craved to be soothed. I felt how sleek the glass was with my other hand, how smooth the wood was at either end as the pile of sand slowly grew higher.

Wait, how could I be so sure it was blood? Blood smelled like iron and rust was a product of iron. Oxidized iron. We had talked about that in science class recently. So it made sense that it smelled like iron. It was probably just rust then, I decided. Maybe I had misunderstood those swirling letters too. Maybe it was something else, a symbol or something.

I flipped the hourglass around again and took another peek at the carvings.

No, they definitely looked like the letters J and W.

J and W like the initials of Jonathan Wilkins, a small voice in my brain whispered, that I instantly shut down. J and W could stand for *a lot* of things. If they even were letters.

It struck me that it would be very odd for an hourglass made of wood and glass to have so much rust on it. There wasn't any rust on the three gold stems that held the two wooden-pieces together. Not only did they look completely rust-free, but they also appeared new.

Why would there be rust on it at all? And all of it on the lower wood plate?

A chill went through me and a renewed wave of nausea rocked my stomach.

Had it been blood on that hourglass then?

The shower shut off in the bathroom, making me wince, and I could hear Mom step out of the bathtub. I dropped the hourglass in the same place where I had found it, then I removed my shoes and jacket and plopped down on the bed.

It didn't take long until the bathroom door opened and Mom appeared in the doorway. She had a white towel wrapped around her body and her butchered black hair was wet. She used a hand towel to dry it, rubbing her scalp hard.

"There you are!" she exclaimed. "I was getting worried

that you had been kidnapped or something." She chuckled lightly. "Seriously, where did you go?"

"I woke up and was super hungry, so I went to the bodega we passed on the way here and bought some... fruit."

She cocked a brow at me. "Fruit? What kind of fruit? The crunchy, fried, salty kind also known as chips and the chewy, colorful kind also known as candy or maybe chocolate?"

Mom was hard to fool.

I waved a dismissive hand, as though that would make her stop questioning me. "Okay, I did buy some of that—"

"With what money?" She put her hands on her hips and narrowed her eyes at me.

"Um..." I shifted in place. "I got some money from your wallet."

"How much?"

"Just like, um, a twenty."

She gazed at me sternly. "Twenty bucks? That's a lot for a snack. Don't do it again. You know we don't have much cash. Next time, ask me first."

"Okay. Sorry."

"That's okay. I'll hurry up and get ready, and then maybe we can go out and find some place where we can have breakfast. That is, if you're still hungry." She glanced at me pointedly.

"I could eat something," I muttered, looking down at my hands.

She walked over to the bed and reached for her tote bag. She paused when she saw the stuff that lay beside it. She reached for the hourglass and handed it to me. I took it from her, confusion written all over my face. *Why is she giving this to me?*

"Pretty, huh? I got that for you," she said casually as she went over to her backpack and pulled out some clothes. I had frozen in place, not sure what to do. "There's some dirt at the bottom. I was going to remove it before giving it to you, but then I forgot all about it. Now it's too late."

She had gotten it for me? From where? And why?

Turning away from me, she pulled on a fresh pair of underwear and a new bra. "You like it, don't you?"

I stared at the shapely thing in my hand, the sand glittering. "Um, yeah, it's very pretty. You—you got it for me? Why?"

"Because I thought you would like it. I just forgot to give it to you. It's an antique. Keep it. It's yours now. When we get home, we can figure out how to clean it. If you still want to. You might not."

I stared at her for a moment as she stuck her head into a navy sweater and slipped it down her body. Next she pulled on a pair of black stretch jeans.

"How about you take a shower and then we go out for breakfast somewhere?" she suggested and rubbed the hand towel in her short hair again. "It's kinda early still, so we should wait a little before we go. There are towels in there that you can use." She nodded toward the bathroom. "They're stiff like cardboard, but that's probably because they've been washed in chlorine so many times. Which is a good thing, considering the place we're in."

"Okay," I said and stuffed the hourglass into my deep hoodie pocket, feeling the letter inside it. Numbly, I walked over to the bathroom and entered it, closing the door behind me. It was warm and wet in there, the mirror covered with steam. I pulled a shirtsleeve over the heel of my hand and wiped some of it off, so I could see myself. I wanted to check if I looked as weird as I was feeling. I couldn't tell. Just that I looked pale like a ghost as always with that ugly, black hair that was getting so long I could soon put it in a small ponytail. What little tan I had gotten in Florida seemed to have turned a dull gray.

Mechanically, I switched on the shower and began to remove my clothes. *She had gotten it for me*? Why? When? And from *where*? And what had she meant by getting it anyway? Buying or stealing it? Did I dare ask?

No, I wasn't going to ask her where she had gotten it, I decided as I stepped under the showerhead, hot streams of water blasting over me. I honestly didn't think she would respond well to such a question. I also didn't think I was ready to deal with the answer. I would never be ready for her answer. I don't know why I thought so, only that I felt certain of it.

I took my time in the shower, carefully washing my hair with the soap provided, and all of my body. Over and over. I felt like I couldn't get clean enough. Something about this whole situation was very disturbing, but I had a hard time putting my finger on exactly what that was. At the moment, all I knew was that I didn't like it and that I would prefer to stay in the shower for many more hours. Forever even. But I couldn't do that; I would have to get out of it and join Mom soon. She would wonder what I was doing otherwise. I couldn't have her suspect me of anything.

I shook my head and laughed. Suspect me of *what?* I wasn't doing anything I shouldn't, and I wasn't about to either. I was just letting my fears and imagination get the best of me. She had nothing to do with Wilkins's murder. Why would she? It was ridiculous for me to even think that for one second. Besides, they already caught the guy who killed him. Today, we would find out more details about that.

I kept chuckling as I soaped up my hair for a third time. Why was I being so silly? *Of course* I should ask her where she had gotten the hourglass. Why would she get mad? She wouldn't. When we had breakfast later, I'd ask her where she had gotten it, why, and what she thought all the dark stains were about.

36

At eight thirty, we went to have breakfast in a small coffee shop several blocks away from the whorehouse, in a much, much nicer area. It turned out we weren't very far from Yorkville, which was a low-key, affordable area where lots of old people lived. The coffee shop we were in was the Mom and Pop kind. Mom loved such places and used every excuse there was to frequent one. On our way to it, we had picked up a copy of the *New York Post,* eager to find out what was going on with the arrested teen. It was a little early, but we still hoped for some fresh news on the situation.

We didn't even check the front page before we had taken a seat inside the coffee shop. (The place was called Gregory's Hot Coffee Shop. Stupid name, right? Who wanted *cold* coffee?) That wasn't for lack of trying, but it was windy and it had begun to rain, which made it very hard to read the paper outside. Our goal had been to keep the paper dry so the ink wouldn't run from the raindrops falling evermore aggressively from the gray sky.

Gregory's Hot Coffee Shop had a surprising amount of people in it, considering the early hour and the bad weather, but we managed to claim a table.

While Mom went to get coffee and tea and blueberry muffins for us to eat and drink, I took a seat at the small table to make sure no one snatched it. I had brought the paper with me and used a few of the paper napkins I got from the cutesy stand on the table to dab it dry. When I was satisfied, I took a look at the front page as I waited for Mom to join me. Some blond chick in a bikini took up half the page. I doubted she was what we were looking for, but I still checked out what followed beneath the headline that said *Killer Crush* in big, bold, black letters.

I was right; this story was about some chick who had stalked and killed her high school crush.

The story I was interested in wasn't even on the front page, but in the bottom half of the fifth page. Once I spotted the headline, I couldn't stop reading:

THE POLICE ARREST THE WRONG PERSON FOR UPPER EAST SIDE PSYCHOLOGIST MURDER.

Spellbound, I kept reading what the article beneath had to say:

Desperate to make progress in the recent Upper East Side murder, the police made the mistake of arresting a former patient of Dr. Jonathan Wilkins on Monday morning. The *arrest was based on an anonymous tip given to the police in which the tipster claimed Nathan Gordon, 16 years old and Dr. Wilkins's former patient, had uttered several death threats to Dr. Wilkins. Some of them had been made directly to Dr. Wilkins's face, according to a witness. Gordon was released early this morning when it was determined that he had not been in the city the night of the murder. Also, the prints on the murder weapon did not belong to him. The police are now refocusing their efforts on finding thirteen-year-old Shane Hanson, who has been on the lam with his mother, Jennifer Hanson, for the last couple of weeks. If you see Shane or Jennifer Hanson, please contact the police at 1 800 577 TIPS immediately. A reward of $10,000 will be paid to the person who has a tip that leads to an arrest. They are considered very....*

I jerked, snapping back to the here and now when Mom pulled out the other chair and took a seat at the table. She placed a tray loaded with coffee, tea, and muffins between us at the same time as the couple right next to us left their table.

"Here you go," she said and smiled at me. The smile on her lips soon shrank and she frowned at me instead. "What's wrong, honey?"

I showed her the newspaper and pointed at the article I had just finished reading. She scanned through it quickly, the furrow between her eyebrows deepening.

"That's not good," she stated casually and put the paper down on the table beside the tray. She had a sip of her coffee, not appearing particularly perturbed. I glared at her. What was wrong with her? How could she appear so calm when we were back to square one, everyone thinking *I* was the killer again?

"Not good?" I repeated incredulously. I leaned toward her and hissed, "Mom, the police think *I* killed Dr. Wilkins!"

She hushed me, glaring back at me now. "Don't talk so loud. There are other people in here. Do you want them to hear what you're saying?" She tossed a few glances left and right, checking out the other patrons. Fortunately, I hadn't spoken that loudly and the nearest person, a girl with purple hair and piercings, wore big headphones, so she had likely not heard a word. She seemed deeply immersed in something on her phone.

"What are we gonna do?" I whispered to Mom, the terror growing inside me. The police thought I had killed Dr. Wilkins. That meant I was going to jail, didn't it? I didn't want to go to jail!

Mom patted my hand. "We're going to tell them it's ridiculous. You couldn't have killed him. You were at home and sleeping deeply in your bed the night he was murdered."

"Yeah, I know, but they still think I did it," I pointed out, stabbing my index finger at the story in question.

She rubbed my arm and whispered, "Honey, calm down. They're only saying that because they're embarrassed and have to say something. They have no other leads."

I just stared at her. How could she remain so calm when

it was so obvious how screwed we were? It said that I was the *focus* of the police investigation. Did she miss that part or what?

"We both know you didn't do it, right?" she continued, unfazed by my reaction.

I banged the table with my fist like a pissed three-year-old. "Yeah, so? *They* don't know that. And I don't want to go to jail!"

"Calm down, Shane. I promise you that you're not going to jail. All this means is that we'll have to remain hidden for a while longer. Until they find the killer. And we may have to help them with that, just like we've already concluded. That's why we came back. Don't worry, it'll all work itself out. You'll see."

"No, it won't. They seem convinced that I'm the killer, Mom. More than ever!"

She squeezed my arm hard then, so hard it hurt. "Shane," she hissed, looking at me sternly. "Please pull yourself together. We're in a public place. There's a reason I'm so certain they won't put you in jail."

"Really? And what's that? Because you really killed him and would take the blame for me?" That had been meant as a joke and I had spoken the words as quietly as I could manage.

"Yes. That is exactly the reason why," Mom responded calmly.

I stared at her, not entirely sure I had heard her correctly.

Did she just confess to me that she had killed Dr. Wilkins, and that she would take the blame for his death was I to get arrested?

"Yes, Shane, I'm the one who did it," she repeated as though she could see straight into my frazzled mind. "I did it to save you. You know there's nothing I wouldn't do to ensure that you're safe, don't you?" This time she grabbed my hand with both of hers instead of squeezing my arm firmly.

I kept staring at her, trying to process what she had just told me. Wait, so *she* had killed Dr. Wilkins? I blinked a couple of times to be sure this wasn't some extremely freaky dream. It clearly wasn't. When I had established that, I waited for her to tell me she was pulling my leg. She had to be pulling my leg. My mom, eccentric or not, wasn't capable of *cold-bloodedly killing* another person. For any reason. The thought was inconceivable. But she kept holding my gaze, her expression steady. She was not about to tell me she was pulling my leg.

Instead she tossed another glance over her shoulder, then whispered, "I had no choice, honey. I knew he would go to the police about what I had told him. I couldn't have that. I had to do something."

"So you—you killed him?" This conversation felt so unreal, like I had been drugged and was just imagining it.

She nodded. "I did it for you. I'd do anything for you, Shane. I love you. You're my son."

She smiled at me, but instead of making me happy she

had done what she claimed to have done, all I could feel was a cold dread.

My mother was a murderer.

37

"Let's leave," she said suddenly. "We can eat this later. We need to talk. I want you to understand why this is all going to work itself out. I don't want you to worry. Let me get a paper bag we can put it in."

Without waiting for me to respond, she got to her feet and left the table, heading for the counter. I watched her as she spoke to the girl behind it, and then how the girl nodded and turned around. When she faced Mom again, there was a brown paper bag in her hands that she gave Mom. Mom returned to the table and calmly began placing the muffins in the bag.

"You can carry your tea, right?" she asked, pointing at the paper cup before me that was full of ginger tea.

I nodded mechanically and put on my coat that I had hung over the chair back. I grabbed my tea cup and walked out of the coffee shop with Mom. It was drizzling outside, but it was no longer windy.

"Where are we going?" I asked her.

"Let's head back to the room," she replied, using the newspaper to shield herself from the rain. I had pulled my coat's hoodie over my head. It did a good job covering both my hair and half of my face, it was so big. *I could definitely use the cover now,* I mused bitterly.

We hurried back to the shady building and entered. Two men and a woman sat on the wicker chairs, talking amongst each other. One of the men was smoking a cigarette and the other drinking a beer directly from the can. They looked like the kind of people you wanted to stay away from. The kind of people my mom would tell me to avoid. Under normal circumstances, that is. Now she seemed like she couldn't care less as we walked by them toward the stairs. It was surreal, though no way near as surreal as her being Dr. Wilkins's killer all along.

I guess she'd taken the cabs to get to his place then. It fit perfectly.

In silence, we hurried up the long, steep stairs to the second floor and walked over to our room. Out of the corner of my eye, I noticed the security camera in the hallway ceiling. Mom unlocked the door and we walked inside. She tossed the paper bag on the unmade bed and removed her coat.

"Brrr," she said and rubbed her arms. "It's cold in here." She squatted next to her backpack and pulled out a sweater that she put on.

Quietly, I removed the hoodie from my head and also removed the jacket. Then I took a seat on the bed, draping the covers around me. It was pretty freezing in the room. I waited for Mom to finish rooting around her backpack and sit down somewhere and tell me why she hadn't told me she had killed Dr. Wilkins all along. I had to know.

Finally, she did take a seat beside me.

"Why didn't you tell me you had killed him right away?" I blurted out before I could think twice about it.

"I didn't want to scare you," she said and grabbed the paper bag from where she had thrown it at the edge of the bed. She opened it and pulled out one of the muffins that she offered me. I flicked a hand no; the last thing I could think of was eating something right now. Not that I had been all that hungry when we'd first headed to breakfast.

"Scare me?" I repeated.

She took a bite of the muffin and started to chew. She held up an index finger, signaling that she would soon tell me more. It felt like she was chewing forever. When she swallowed, she grabbed a bottle of water and had a large gulp from it.

Wiping her mouth with the back of her hand, she said, "Yes. I didn't want to scare you. I can tell that you're scared right now. Imagine if I would've told you right away what I had done? I don't think you would have been able to handle it. No, I thought it was much better if I kept quiet. To tell you the truth, I hoped that I would never have to tell you at all. I was counting on someone being arrested fairly rapidly and then *remaining* arrested. A long-practicing psychologist like Dr. Wilkins usually has lots of people who want to hurt him or her. Like after a week or so I expected someone to be arrested. That way you would never have had to find out the truth. It would have been so much better." She reached out a hand and ran a knuckle over my cheek, gazing at me tenderly like she so often did. "Trust me, I never wanted to let you know the truth. I knew it would be very upsetting for you."

"So what was your plan? For us to be on the lam forever? I mean, if you're the killer, they'll never find the killer. Or they'll keep thinking I'm the killer, which they seem to be doing now. Did you use our Crate & Barrel knife to kill him?"

"No, I used one of his knives. I took it from his kitchen. I'm not so stupid I'd use one of *our* knives, honey!" She chuckled and had another bite of the muffin. I just looked at her, not feeling like laughing at all. I couldn't believe how she could be so laid-back about the fact that she had stabbed a man to death. How she could just sit there and eat a blueberry muffin.

"And obviously we wouldn't be on the lam forever," she continued. "Only until they caught the killer."

What was she talking about? *She* was the killer.

"The man I had set up to be the killer, that is," she added, placing a hand on my arm. "I have this all planned out, you see. I have the perfect guy to take the blame for Wilkins's death. The perfect fall guy."

"Really? And who's that?"

Her face darkened and she gazed beyond me, out the window, at the rain beating the pane. "A really, really bad person."

"A really bad person?"

"Yes." She faced me again. "One of his patients. A man who brutally raped and killed a woman. His ex-wife. I figured I might as well kill two birds with one stone. I used the same size shoes that man wears when I went to Wilkins's house, and I also left a watch that belongs to him in the house." She frowned lightly. "It's surprising the police haven't found him yet. I was sure it was him they had arrested when we found out that someone had been caught." She shook her head forlornly. "Too bad it was someone else. But that's okay. We'll leave an anonymous tip for the cops so they can get the man finally. By tomorrow they'll have arrested him for sure. Forget about you being their number one suspect and so dangerous. Like I said, that's just something the cops made up so they can look tough and on top of things."

"Really?"

She smiled. "Yes, really. I told you you have a lot to learn about life. Cops do dirty things like that *all the time.*"

"Huh. But why didn't we do that right away? I mean, why didn't you tell the cops about him? Why did we run away, so the cops got all suspicious, thinking *I* killed Wilkins?"

She glanced at me for a long silent moment. "One day I hope I can tell you why. I don't think it's a good idea to do it now. Trust me, it was all to protect you. Everything I do is to keep you safe. Please trust me on that one. You do, don't you, honey?"

I nodded automatically.

She ruffled my hair. "That's good. How about we meditate now?"

"Um, okay. Just please answer this question first: How did you even find out that this man raped and killed his ex-wife?"

Much to my surprise, Mom suddenly blushed and she averted her gaze.

"Are you okay?" I asked her.

Reluctantly, she met my eyes. "I really wish I didn't have to tell you this, but I don't see how else I can explain why I know the truth about this man. You see, Dr. Wilkins and I were more than patient and therapist, honey. We were lovers too. One day he told me about this man in his thirties he had just started treating who had confessed his horrible crime to him. And how horrible it was for him that he wasn't allowed to tell the police about it."

This was just getting weirder and weirder. Mom had been *sleeping* with Dr. Wilkins? When did *that* start? "You mean because he's not allowed to?"

"Exactly. So you see this man deserves to be set up for

this crime. He's a bad person who should not be able to get away with what he's done."

38

A few hours later, I told Mom that I was going to go out for some fresh air. She would remain in the room and rest for a while.

I didn't need fresh air as much as I needed some time on my own. Some time to think away from Mom. The more time I spent with her, the more uncomfortable I got. Something was wrong with her. Seriously wrong. It was like she was going crazy. Crazy with a capital C and an exclamation mark. Her eyes were bulging and she hardly blinked. She was talking fast and seemed agitated despite us having meditated. Well, at least *she* had meditated. I had just been sitting there beside her on the bed, counting the seconds until we were supposed to be done. There was no way I'd be able to relax next to her now. Not after all that she had confessed to me.

She had friggin' *killed* Dr. Wilkins—whom she'd apparently been *dating* in secret. I was still having a hard time imagining her with the balding man with the double-chin and weird glasses who I had seen in several pictures online and on TV. It just didn't fit. And that story she had told me about setting up his rapist/ex-wife killer patient had sounded so bizarre. Boy, had that sounded nutty! And this was even weirder: I thought the reason she had felt she absolutely had to kill Dr. Wilkins was because she had been sure he'd tell the cops about me, have them arrest me for killing Alice because of the pics in my phone. (Which I've now deleted, obviously. I should never have taken them in the first place.)

But if Dr. Wilkins could tell about me, why couldn't he also tell the cops about the rapist/murderer? That didn't make sense at all. Plus, if she had been sleeping with Dr. Wilkins, why would he be so mean and run to the police about her son? You'd think he'd cut her some slack if he wanted to keep sleeping with her. My mom, before she cut all her hair and dyed it black and started wearing those ugly fake glasses, was very pretty. Guys often checked her out. She was a catch for a dude like Dr. Wilkins. Even I, who was only thirteen, knew getting your girl's son in trouble was not a smart move if you wanted to keep her happy.

I shook my head and tsk-tsked. Nothing made sense here. I picked up my pace and pulled the hoodie farther down my face. I didn't feel like being recognized by some money-hungry individual. In the article from this morning, it had said that you would get a big reward if you helped the cops arrest me. I remembered that very clearly.

I sighed heavily. This was *such* a shit show. I needed to fix it somehow. It didn't look like Mom had the situation under control at all.

It was a regular weekday in December, which meant the public library should be open. There were lots of branches in the city; if I kept walking downtown, I should bump into one soon. I would be able to do some research at the public library. For example, I was dying to find out if my hunch was right. A psychologist had to be able to report a rapist and a murderer, right? I looked left and right in search of a library I could use.

It took me about twenty minutes before I found one, about thirty blocks away from the whorehouse. Thankfully, it was open. I hurried inside and found a free computer instantly. Opening a browser, I typed in the search phrases "professional secrecy" and "psychologist". Several options appeared on the screen. I clicked on a few of the links and read through the corresponding articles. *Hmm.* It appeared my hunch had been wrong, which meant Mom had been correct, which was a relief in a way. Her story made more sense now. Apparently, a psychologist was *not* allowed to break his professional secrecy if his or her patient confessed to a crime such as murder and rape—as long as the crime had taken place in the past and there was no reason to fear the perpetrator would do it again.

Mom must have told Dr. Wilkins that she thought I was a danger to society. Based on what she had told me, that's what it had sounded like anyway. I nodded to myself; it had *definitely* sounded like that. No wonder she had been so worried Dr. Wilkins would tell the cops about me. So worried that she had seen no other option but to kill him. She must have totally panicked, not been able to think clearly.

All of a sudden, I remembered what she had said about the teen the NYPD had arrested yesterday. How she had been convinced it had been the rapist/ex-wife killer: *"It's surprising the police haven't found him yet. I was sure it was him they had arrested when we found out that someone had been caught."*

But the man she had referred to had not only been married, but he had also been in his thirties, according to Mom. How could she have been so sure it was him the cops had arrested? They had clearly stated they had arrested a teenager, not a man. She must have lied about that then. Why did she lie about that?

Obviously, they wouldn't think the rapist/murderer guy was the killer just because she had used the same size shoes as he wore and left his watch at Dr. Wilkins's place. I couldn't remember having read anything about the cops having found a strange watch or mentioning the killer's shoe size. By the way, how the heck did she even *know* what size shoes that dude wore, and how the heck had she gotten her hands on his watch? Had she dated him too or what? I laughed that seemed so ridiculous.

I swallowed hard and chewed on my thumbnail. This was so not good. Nothing made sense.

Part of me wanted to go back and confront Mom, but another, much bigger part, felt terrified going back home and facing her again. She seemed like she was about to snap any second. Wait, maybe she already had snapped. I mean, she had just confessed to killing Dr. Wilkins after all... Oh God. I sighed heavily. What the hell should I *do?* My mom was a friggin' killer. I didn't want to talk to her again, even be around her, but I didn't know what else to do but to go back to that crappy room. It wasn't like I could go to the police. They would just put me in jail. The mere thought of going to jail made me shiver with terror.

I suddenly felt how my eyes brimmed over with hot tears. Something was seriously wrong with Mom. I could feel it in my entire body. What was wrong with her? I tried to stifle my sniffles and wiped at my eyes with the sleeve of my hoodie Wait, maybe I could go to Grandma and tell her what was going on. But what if she didn't believe me? What if she thought I had killed Dr. Wilkins like the cops so clearly believed? Yeah, she'd probably think that. She had no reason to doubt the cops. I pictured her yelling at me, her and Grandpa taking me to the cops, and it made me cry harder.

I felt a hand on my shoulder then, which made me jerk. The hand flew off me and a woman said, "I'm so sorry, I didn't mean to scare you."

Slowly, I turned toward the voice. A gray-haired woman with round glasses who was maybe sixty-five stood beside me, watching me with a concerned expression on her wrinkled face.

"I just wanted to see if there was something I could do to help," she said softly. "You seem upset. I work here at the library."

I kept crying, unable to control myself or talk. The woman put her hand on my shoulder and led me to a quiet corner in the library with lots of big plants in pots. She sat down on a wooden bench between the plants and made me sit down, too.

She produced some paper napkins from her pants pocket that she handed me. Without a word, I took them and wiped my wet cheeks. She waited several beats before she spoke again.

"Do you want to tell me what's wrong?"

I took a few deep breaths, then stuttered, "I think my mom is going crazy."

She peered at me through the thick glasses. "Your mom is going crazy? Where is your mom?"

I sighed. "At this place in East Harlem. In a shady building." For some reason, I didn't want to add that the building in question was really a whorehouse. Well, I guessed it wasn't an actual whorehouse, but it was close enough and I didn't know how else to describe it.

"What is she doing there?"

"Hiding. She and I are hiding." I blew my nose.

"You're hiding? From what?"

"The police. They're after us. Mom did something bad. It's a long story."

My burner phone went off in my pocket then. It had to be

Mom. She was the only person who knew my number. It kept ringing and ringing.

"Are you going to answer that?" the old woman asked kindly.

Not knowing what else to do, I reached for the phone in my pocket and pressed the Talk button. I cleared my throat before saying, "Hello."

"Shane? Where are you? You've been gone a long time. Are you okay?"

"Yes, I'm fine, Mom. I'm at the library."

"At the library? What library?"

"Some library on the Upper East Side."

"What are you doing there?"

"Research."

"Oh. Why don't you come back home now, honey?" It was clear she didn't mean that as a question. It was an order. A chill went through me. The last thing I wanted was to go back to Mom. Something was very wrong with her. Had she started drinking in secret again? That would explain a lot of things. If she was secretly drunk. Not that I had smelled any alcohol on her breath, but you could hide that. Mom was an expert at hiding such stuff.

"Okay," I said just to say something. "See you soon."

We said goodbye and hung up.

"Was that your mom?" the woman asked.

"Yes. She wants me to come back to the room. But I'm too scared to go back there on my own. It's a bad place." I sighed heavily and blew my nose again with the paper napkin. I honestly didn't know what to do. I had to go back at some point. The police wanted me. I didn't want to go to prison.

"I can go with you if you want," the lady suggested and gazed at me warmly. "My name is Betty. I just finished my shift. I'm one of the librarians. I was on my way home anyway."

"You can?" I stared at her. I could go back if this lady came with me. She seemed really nice. I didn't think Mom would like it, but I didn't care. There was no way I was going back there on my own. I didn't want to be alone with Mom any longer. Not if she was crazy *and* drunk. The more I considered her having secretly started drinking again, the more convinced I was she had in fact been drunk all the time lately. Maybe Betty could talk to her, figure out why she was behaving so crazily. It was worth a try.

"Yes, I can," she said and smiled. She got to her feet. "Why don't we go now?"

"Okay," I said and got to my feet. My coat was still hanging over the chair at the computer table, so we went over there and got it. Then Betty went to get her own coat and her purse.

A couple of minutes later, we were on our way back to the whorehouse.

39

T he sun had gone down and it was getting dark out by the time Betty and I reached the whorehouse. I had managed to calm down and come to my senses as she and I were walking. It had dawned on me that it was not a good idea for me to tell this lady that Mom had killed Dr. Wilkins. After all, she had done it to protect me. Yeah, it was crazy, but still. It had been for my sake. Maybe Mom knew things I didn't about Dr. Wilkins. Maybe she had been dating the rapist/ex-wife killer, too, which was how she had gotten hold of his watch and seen his shoe size. Yes, that was probably how it had all gone down. Wilkins would for sure have told the police that he thought I had killed Alice when I hadn't. Betty didn't know all that, so she would probably go straight to the police and tell them Mom was crazy. I couldn't let her do that. I didn't want Mom to go to prison either. Not even for a day. Instead, I needed to figure out on my own why she was behaving so strangely, saying so many things that didn't make sense. Why she had been lying to me about thinking the teen the cops had arrested was the rapist/killer. I had to be absolutely *sure* it all had to do with the drinking, not just assume so because it was convenient. Hopefully, Betty could help with that last part, the drinking part. I didn't think she'd run to the police just because Mom was a closet alcoholic. Either way, I would make sure she didn't stay long. It was not smart to drag other people into this.

As we were about to enter the building, it struck me that maybe Mom had simply not *known* that Wilkins could have gone to the police regarding the rapist/ex-wife killer. Maybe he had told her that he couldn't for some special reason and she had believed him. Maybe Wilkins was an evil bastard like his patient. It was all very possible.

I had probably overreacted here.

I was definitely regretting having brought Betty, but it was too late now. We were already walking into the dimly lit lobby where there were a couple of new people seated on the old wicker set. Two middle-aged men in business suits. Probably johns, I mused.

I'll just have her meet Mom and tell her that I'm fine now, I thought as we climbed the steep stairs up to the second floor. Thank her for walking me home. Hopefully, Mom wouldn't be drunk and act weird or something. Look normal. I had already told Betty that I had been exaggerating the fact that Mom had done something bad. I told Betty that all Mom had done was getting fired from her job and then getting us evicted, which was why we were staying at this crappy place. It was only until she could figure out how to get a new job. That wasn't a crime. Yes, hopefully Mom would behave like a normal person and then Betty would just leave.

"It's here," I told the librarian and walked up to the door to our room. I knocked lightly on it before I opened it, praying Mom was looking presentable. She had no idea I wasn't coming alone.

She was seated on the edge of the bed, reading something when we entered. The smile on her face instantly died when she saw that I was with someone. She stared at Betty and I knew bringing her here had been a bad idea. A very bad idea. But it was too late now. I'd just make up some story to Mom later, tell her Betty had insisted on walking me home. Which wasn't a total lie.

"Hi, Mom," I said after Betty and I had entered the room. "This is Betty. She works at the library where I went. She wanted to make sure I got back to you all right."

"Hello," Betty said to Mom, who had gotten to her feet. She was wearing the same jeans and dark sweater as before, but also sneakers on her feet.

"Hello," Mom said and a strained smile stretched her lips. "Thanks for looking out for my son. I was so worried he'd gotten lost. It's no city for kids to walk around in alone. I'm Jennifer."

I paused when I heard her use her real name. Was that really smart? We had decided we would tell everyone we were called Joey and Rita. Mom walked up to us and extended a hand to Betty. The old woman took it and they shook hands.

"I apologize for the mess here," Mom said and indicated the room, which was pretty messy, I noted for the first time. "I was about to go out to pick up some coffee. Why don't we go to the coffee shop down the street and have some coffee and something sweet to eat? My treat since you were so kind and made sure my son got back to me safely. I was terrified something had happened to him." She smiled warmly at Betty.

"Sure, that sounds like a good idea," Betty said and opened the door to leave. I followed her and Mom did, too, grabbing her coat from a hook on the wall on the way. Mom told us to keep walking, so Betty and I continued toward the stairs, ahead of Mom, who was locking the door. Betty couldn't walk very fast, though, so we had barely reached the top of the stairs before Mom caught up with us.

As Betty and I were about to descend the stairs, Mom suddenly used her fists to shove Betty hard in the back so she fell down the stairs. Letting out a terrified scream, the old woman tumbled downward at a scary pace that somehow still felt like slow motion. She rolled over a couple of times before she reached the bottom. The back of her head banged hard into the stone floor and she lay motionless, face up. Her glasses were gone from her nose.

Before I could say anything, Mom turned to me where we had remained at the top of the stairs. Her face was twisted with anger and she whispered, "What were you thinking bringing that woman here? *Huh?*"

My eyes went between her and Betty much farther down on the floor. The librarian remained disturbingly silent and motionless, the blood streaming out in every direction from her gray-haired head.

Mom didn't wait for me to say anything; instead, she rushed down the stairs toward Betty. Not knowing what else to do, I hurried after her just in time to catch the two men in business suits rushing out of the lobby. They clearly didn't want to be associated with what had just happened. The woman in the hole in the wall stared at the scene, as though she had frozen in place, her eyes large and her face ashen with shock.

First Mom, then I crouched next to Betty, who suddenly opened her eyes and muttered something unintelligible. Mom swiftly placed her hands at the sides of the woman's head and whispered, "What did you say?"

She leaned over Betty's face at the same time as she twisted the old woman's head discreetly so it snapped, using the heels of her hands. The crunching sound of bone breaking was nauseating, quiet but nonetheless distinct.

I stared at Mom, so shocked at what she had just done that I was speechless. She had just broken the woman's *neck*. She was clearly meaning business here. Would she come after me next? Panicked, I tossed a glance over at the hole in the wall and noticed that the woman in there was gone. Had she seen what had just happened? I had no idea. All I knew was that I had to get the hell away from Mom, who had snapped many times over. There was a ferocious glint in her eyes as she looked at me, which made me pop to my feet in terror.

"She's dead," Mom wailed then. "Oh my God, she's dead! Someone help us. Oh, my God. Oh, my *God!*"

As fast as I could, I dashed out of the lobby, my mom's wailing voice ringing in my ears. I sprinted down the street at breakneck speed, nearly crashing into a man and a woman who seemed to be on their way into the building.

I kept running and running, my legs flying through the air. Running and running and running, bumping into people on the way. Tripping and falling a couple of times. Crashing to the ground. Each time I was instantly back on my feet, though, back to running as fast as I could manage. I had to get as far away as I could from Mom.

At some point much later, I ran out of juice. I sank down on a bench at a bus stop, catching my breath and trying to gather my thoughts. I kept blinking my eyes, digging my nails into my palms so hard the skin must have broken. This must be a dream, just a terrible dream. It had to be. But why wasn't I waking up then? Why did it all feel so real?

Oh God. It's because it *was* all real.

40

I don't know how long I remained seated on that bench, only that it must have been a while. At some point I pushed myself to my feet, though. My mouth felt dry and I was thirsty. I needed something to drink. Soon. I could get that at a police station. I had no choice but to go to the police now and tell them my mom was totally crazy. A crazy murderer. It was sad but true. I still loved her, but that didn't make her any less of a crazy murderer. They needed to stop her before she could kill more people. She clearly had no problem killing people. A shiver ran through me.

Unfortunately, I didn't know where I was or where the nearest police station was located. I looked left and right and all I could see was buildings, most of them apartments, a lot of them with storefronts on the bottom floor. A few people walked by on the dark street, all of them ignoring me. A bus went by on the road and several cars drove by as well. I thought I was somewhere in midtown on the eastside, but I couldn't be sure. Maybe I was still in Yorksville. I honestly had no idea how long I had been running. It felt like forever, but maybe it only felt like that. Everything looked the same to me here. Not that it really mattered. I could always ask someone if they knew where there was a police station. The nearest one couldn't be that far away.

I kept walking down the street and after a few minutes, I spotted a police car driving slowly along the road. *Great,* I thought, not particularly excited. They would know where the nearest station was. I made a sharp turn and ran into the road to wave them down. The officers in the car would help me, take me straight to a police station where I could drink something and tell them everything. Have them arrest Mom. She was too dangerous to be walking around on the streets on her own. I waved my arms frantically in front of the car until they saw me.

The police cruiser drove up to the side of the road and the cop on the passenger side, a tough-looking black woman, got out.

"Hi there," she said and walked up to me. "Can I help you?"

"Yes, please," I said and inhaled deeply; I was more out of breath than I had thought apparently. "I need you to help me. My mom is a killer. She is killing people. Something's seriously wrong with her, but I don't know what. You need to stop her. Help me stop her. She's acting very crazy."

The police officer looked me up and down, then asked me what my name was.

"My name's Shane Hanson," I replied eagerly. "My mom's name is Jennifer Hanson. She's gone crazy."

The officer nodded, then told me to come with her to the car so we could head to the station where we could talk more. She opened the back door and ushered me inside. Then she got into the front passenger seat and we took off. There was plexi glass between the front and the back-seat, which was pretty roomy. I imagined that lots of crooks had been sitting here before me. Not that I was a crook or anything.

I looked out the window at all the cars driving by. These cops seemed to know exactly what to do next, which wasn't exactly surprising. (I mean, they were cops, right? This situation must be pretty routine for them.) I allowed myself to relax and leaned back into the car seat, closing my eyes. Thank God this police car had driven down the road. I honestly didn't think I would have been able to keep going for much longer. Finally I would be able to talk to some sane people, get back to safety.

An image of Betty lying on the stoneground inside the whorehouse, limp like a ragdoll, filled my head then. I could see her open her eyes, the glasses gone. She looked all dazed, her eyelids fluttering, and then I could hear her mutter something that had sounded like "help me", but it could have been something else. Before I could say anything, Mom's hands had been on Betty's head and she had discreetly snapped the poor woman's neck, producing that terrible crunching sound that had sent chills up my spine.

Letting out a gasp, I opened my eyes, forcing the disturbing pictures and sounds out of my mind. I stared out the windshield window instead, between the front seats' headrests, then grabbed hold of the seats and pulled myself forward.

"Are you taking me to the station?" I asked the female officer through the glass, hoping she could hear me. Best to be sure we were going to the right place.

"Yes," she replied, tossing a glance over her shoulder in my direction. "We'll get there in about five minutes. You'll be able to tell us your whole story then."

"Good," I replied and leaned back again. "It's a crazy story. Like, really crazy."

"It usually is," she commented, her eyes on the road again.

It didn't take long until we pulled into a small parking lot behind the station. The cops opened the door, and the female one opened my door and asked me to step out. I did as I was told and walked with the cops through the parking lot. Neither of them said anything as they walked on either side of me. We reached the street and the glass doors that led into the police station. There was a counter in the lobby behind which another policewoman sat.

A door suddenly opened and a man and a woman in regular clothes entered the lobby.

"That's Shane Hanson?" the man asked one of the officers.

"Yes," the woman answered.

"Good job. Cuff him and bring him into interrogation room two."

I heard the sound of metal clinking as the male officer removed his cuffs from his belt, and then I felt cold metal wrap around my wrists. He pulled the cuffs so tightly my skin hurt, and then I heard a clicking sound as they locked.

What the hell is going on here?

I looked at the female officer, who had remained by my side, silent and immobile.

"What—what are you doing?" I asked her, the panic growing inside me. "Why are you putting handcuffs on me? I think you're misunderstanding. I'm not the bad guy. It's my *mom* who's the killer. I know the NYPD thinks I killed Dr. Wilkins, but I didn't. I promise. *She* did. She told me so this morning. And just now she pushed a librarian who was trying to help me down the stairs to her death. I can show you where the body is. I stopped you on the road so you could help me stop *her*. Why are—"

The male officer brusquely pushed me toward the door the plain-clothed man was holding. I had no choice but to walk in that direction. Or stumble was more like it.

What the hell was going on? What were they doing to

me? Why was I wearing handcuffs like some friggin' *criminal?* I wasn't the killer. My mom was the killer, the bad person. Well, at least the *crazy* person. The crazy *killer person.* Why were they treating me like I was one, too? Oh God, they must think I *helped* her…

They were pushing me through a long hallway and then into a room with a gray table and a few steel chairs. Another man in regular clothes was there, as well as… *Mom.*

As we stopped in the middle of the room, I stared at Mom, who was seated beside that man. I was unable to get a word out, I was so stunned. I noticed then that her face was swollen and her eyes red like she had been crying. Wait, she was still crying. She wiped at her face with some tissue.

Okay, what the hell was going *on?* Why was she here and crying? And why wasn't she wearing handcuffs?

"Is that him?" the man beside her asked. He had big sideburns and a handlebar mustache.

"Yes…" she stuttered. "That's him. Oh God…" An onslaught of tears overcame her, and she buried her face in fresh tissues that she got from the Kleenex box in her lap.

The man beside her helped her up to her feet, and then she and Mustache Man left the room. She avoided meeting my gaze.

I was taken to the seat behind the table and forced to sit down there.

The man and the woman in the regular clothes took a seat on the chairs on the other side of the table.

The man leaned toward me and said, "My name is Detective Lou Pedersen. This is my colleague, Detective Eve Cruz. Do you know why you're here?"

"No!" I exclaimed, terrified now. Something was really, really wrong here, and it felt like it was about to get worse. Much worse. "Why are you doing this to me? You're supposed to put the handcuffs on my mom. *She's* the crazy one. Not me."

"Calm down, Shane," Detective Pedersen ordered me sternly. "You can't play us, so give it a rest. Your manipulative ways won't work here. We know all about what you've done. How many people you've killed in your short life. What you're up to. See, we're used to little bastards like you. Psychopathic monsters. Though, I have to say, you're the best one I've met so far." He stroked his square chin and studied me for a moment. "You do come across as a perfectly normal kid. A nice one even."

I stared at him, feeling like throwing up. *We know all about what you've done. How many people you've killed in your short life. What you're up to. See, we're used to little bastards like you. Psychopathic monsters.* What was happening here? Why was he saying all these nasty things to me? The cops were supposed to *help* me! My eyes filled with angry tears that crawled down my face. Why was this happening to me? It had to be a bad dream. But I didn't think it was. It seemed much too real.

The two detectives contemplated me in silence for several

seconds during which I felt increasingly sick and dizzy. These detectives had somehow gotten the idea that *I* was the one who'd killed Wilkins and maybe even Betty, too. I suddenly remembered how Mom had thrown a glance over her shoulder in the hallway, then quickly shoved the old woman down the stairs. I remembered how she had cried and cried, glaring at me like it was *my fault* she had pushed Betty down the stairs. But why would she do that? It wasn't *my fault* that she had decided to push Betty, then broken her neck. Why was she blaming *me?*

A woman entered the room and placed a Coke can on the table, then left again.

"Are you thirsty, Shane?" Detective Cruz asked me and opened the can.

I was extremely thirsty I realized then. "Yes," I mumbled.

She gave the other detective a nod, who got to his feet and came up behind me. He unlocked the cuffs. Leaving one of the cuffs around my wrist, he placed the other around the table leg and clicked it shut.

Detective Cruz shoved the Coke toward me. "Drink."

I used my free hand and chugged the can's contents as quickly as I could, then put the empty can back on the table.

"Why is Mom not here with me?" I asked her. I had a vague feeling that the parents had to be with minors like me if they got in trouble with the police. I had seen it on TV many times. So why had Mom just left me here? She was supposed to protect me, wasn't she?

"She told us we have her permission to ask you anything we want without her presence," Detective Cruz replied calmly. "She's terrified of you and has finally accepted the fact that you don't belong among regular folks. You need to be kept away from them. And we will help her achieve that."

41

I don't know what came over me, but I suddenly started laughing. This situation was so incredibly preposterous that I didn't know what to say or do any longer. Mom was scared of *me?*

How could she be scared of me? *She* was the crazy one! How had she managed to convince the police I was crazy when *she* was? This was insane!

Well, when they heard my story, they would understand what was going on. They would understand that she, for some inexplicable reason, was determined to have me take the blame for what she had done. All that she had done. She must have been drunk or something. It was the only thing that made sense now. The alcohol had made her snap.

"You think this is funny, don't you?" Detective Cruz commented sarcastically. She glanced over at her colleague. "Why am I not surprised, Lou?"

"Why did you decide to kill Dr. Jonathan Wilkins?" Detective Pedersen asked me, leaning toward me.

I was so stunned that they thought I had killed that guy that I didn't know what to say. I just looked at them, from one to the other. Didn't they *see* how crazy Mom was? How could they not? It was so obvious.

"Why did you decide to kill Dr. Wilkins?" Detective Pedersen repeated, glaring at me, demanding an answer.

"I didn't kill him," I muttered, glancing down at my hands now. "Mom killed him. She told me so this morning. She did it to protect me. She loves me and will do anything to protect me. Ask her yourself. Later. She must be drunk or something right now. Something has made her go crazy. That's why she told me we had to leave the city. Because the cops had somehow gotten the idea that *I* had killed Dr. Wilkins. I didn't. She did. To protect me."

"Really?" Detective Cruz said and crossed her arms over her ample chest. "Well, I guess *that* part is true. That she wanted to protect you at every cost in the beginning. We did read the letter she sent Detective Ivan Morales. She was very worried about your mental health. At the time, she did want to protect you because she thought you were *innocent.*" She gave me a dry smile that looked more like a smirk. "You had her fooled, didn't you? Just like you had everyone else in your life fooled. Except for Dr. Wilkins. You knew he was too smart, that he would see through your charades. You knew he was going to go to the cops and tell them what a threat to society you are. How you needed to be taken off the streets before you could kill more people like your dad and your friend

Alice. That poor old woman. But you decided to put a stop to that before he could do any harm. And when I say put a stop, I mean *put a stop.*"

I stared at her, amazed at the words that were coming out of her mouth. Wait, Mom had sent the letter to Detective Morales? So what was that other letter, with the empty sheet, all about then?

"You borrowed your mom's credit card and took a cab from your house in Queens to the Upper East Side building where Dr. Wilkins lived," Detective Pedersen continued, smoothly transitioning his colleague's accusations. "You didn't realize that her credit card statements would show not only that you had used the card for cab rides, but also which day, even *time.*" He chuckled and shook his head. "For a brilliant psychopath, you are pretty stupid, I have to say. Why the hell would you use a knife from your own house to stab the psychologist? Who does something like that?" He sent Detective Cruz a glance. "You were really lucky that Dr. Wilkins was in the habit of not locking his front door at night, weren't you? I doubt you would have gotten inside otherwise. Because you're not all that bright after all, are you?"

I opened my mouth to say something, but Detective Cruz cut me off before anything could come out.

"Or maybe you're just a reckless person who likes to play things by ear," she said. "Go with the flow, see what happens. Maybe you hadn't really planned on killing Dr. Wilkins that night, but then it turned out that his effing *front door had been left open,* so how could you not? It was like a sign from heaven, a sign that you had to go through with what you had planned to do. So you did. Too bad someone saw you leave the building after you had stabbed poor Dr. Wilkins to death." She gave another smirk. "Too bad you left the knife behind with all your fingerprints on it. I have to ask, why did you do that? Did you want us to know you were the killer all along? You did, didn't you? Because you thought that, even if we had the murder weapon with all your fingerprints on it, we wouldn't be able to arrest you. We wouldn't be able to get to you. Well, you were wrong, weren't you?"

I was literally speechless, not to mention about to throw up. It was slowly dawning on me that Mom was behind all of this. She must have changed her mind at the last second and decided that she didn't want to take the blame after all. Better the cops thought I was the killer all along.

Detective Cruz took a seat at the edge of the table. "What I don't understand is why you had to kill that sweet old lady, Betty McLaren. What had she done to you to deserve such an end? Why did you have to push her down all those stairs? Huh?"

"I didn't push her," I muttered. "Mom pushed her, then she broke her neck when she saw she wasn't dead after all."

The two detectives exchanged a glance. "Wow," Detective Cruz said. "Just, *wow*. You're still gonna blame *Mom* after all she's done for you, trying to help you? After having killed her husband? You know that she'll be punished for taking you away, don't you? She was harboring a fugitive. She could do up to five years in prison for that. Don't you think it's time to cut your mom some slack now?" She cocked a brow at me.

"Mom gave me an hourglass that I think is Dr. Wilkins's," I said, having suddenly remembered that I had it in my pocket. And that there had been video cameras in both our room and in the whorehouse's hallways. If the cops saw what was on the tapes, they would see that the hourglass had been in Mom's tote bag all along, not to mention how *Mom* had been the one to push and kill Betty. "You should be able to see it falling out of her bag in our room at the... brothel." I really didn't know what else to call it. "There were cameras there. And there were cameras outside in the hallway too. In the lobby area too. You can check them and then you'll know I'm telling the truth. I didn't kill Dr. Wilkins or Betty. She did. She told me. Check the cameras."

"We were told there are cameras in the building where you were," Detective Pedersen stated, holding my gaze. "Very old ones. Unfortunately, someone had cut the cords behind the ones in your room and in the hallway the morning after you got there, rendering those cameras useless. You know anything about that?"

42

It all went much smoother than I could ever have imagined it going. Shane would go to juvenile prison where he'd be totally fucked up by the time they'd let him get out. That is, if they ever let him out. I really doubted he'd last very long in such a rough environment. At the very least, as pretty as he was, he'd be someone's bitch, take it in the ass every night. I couldn't help but wonder if whoever claimed him would be disappointed when they realized Shane wasn't a virgin. Peter had already taken care of that. I had watched him take our son using various objects with my own eyes more than once. (He had even tried to use his dick, but that had been much too big for Shane to handle.) Not that the kid had ever seen me, having his face buried in a pillow all the while.

My heart clenched with pain when I thought of Peter, and how our bastard son had killed him in cold blood. I knew it had been on purpose all along. *Of course* it had been on purpose. Too bad it was too hard to make anyone buy that without also having to admit that Peter had played with Shane, making Shane hate him. So I had pretended like it had been an accident instead. It was safer. I knew I'd get my revenge eventually anyway. I was anything but impatient. For years I had been waiting for the right time, the right opportunity to build on. Finally, when I found the pics of dead Alice in his phone, I knew I had found it.

I smiled to myself as I watched myself in the bathroom mirror in our house. For a thirty-nine-year-old woman, soon to be forty, I thought I looked pretty good, even though my blond hair was still on the short side. I still had no wrinkles around my eyes—well, only when I laughed hard, but that didn't count, did it? Everybody got crow's feet then. Nor did I have any bags under my nice green eyes. I could hardly wait until I was able to grow out my hair all the way and I would look like myself again. I had great hair. The men would all ogle me then. I was far from over the hill yet. I made a point to stay out of the sun, which bought me more time. More time to be pretty. Looking good was an advantage. During our years killing people together, Peter and I had made good use of the fact that we were both attractive, wholesome-looking people. No one ever suspected us of anything iffy despite that we had a dozen murders under our belts before Shane was even born. The cops didn't even suspect that I had been involved in my own brother's murder, even though I had been at the bar the night Peter had beaten him to death. Yes, I had been the "girlfriend" my asshole pervert of a brother had bothered.

Well, he sure got what he deserved in the end, didn't he? He sure did. As often as I could, I went to his grave and pissed on it. That didn't happen nearly as often as I would have liked, sadly. Only a few times a year.

People could be such idiots. Yet again, I had proven this to myself. I had managed to get my son in jail, most likely for forever. As I already told you, I really doubted he would get out at eighteen. The judge had given him the option to get out then, if he showed enough progress. See, they had given him a therapist to work with him while he was in juvy. If he seemed like he had improved enough to be around regular people by age eighteen, they would let him out.

If he didn't kill himself at some point—I was almost one hundred percent certain he would kill himself—I would make sure to break him down myself during my visits. I knew just what to do to make that happen. I'd pay some other imprisoned bastard to help me make that happen if need be. There was no way my son would ever get out of prison. He would rot in prison. Rot like Peter had been doing in his grave.

Maybe the best part of this whole experience was the fact that I'd be able to make a lot of money on my story. I had already been on several talk shows during which I had been discussing my son and the fact that he was a bonafide psychopath. It didn't take long until I was offered a million dollars by a Hollywood movie company for the rights to my script that I'd been working on. When I was interviewed on TV, I made sure to tell the hosts that I had been using writing as therapy, writing about my experiences with my son.

Writing was the only thing that kept me sane these days, I claimed with tears in my eyes.

It wasn't therapy at all. I knew all along that it would make a great story, a great movie, a great *marketable* movie after I had been on a few talk shows. So I'd started writing the screenplay as soon as Shane had been arrested. It took me only a week to complete it. I'd written day and night, like a maniac. I barely slept at all. I named it *Born Evil*. Great title, huh?

The movie execs said they think they'll have Scarlett Johansen playing me. I'm not sure about that. She wasn't pretty enough and she had a big ass, too. I'd much rather have someone like Gwyneth Paltrow playing me. A much younger version, obviously.

You didn't buy that my son had things wrong with his brain, did you? He doesn't. Well, not as far as *I* know at least. Maybe he does. Peter and I never had his brain checked. But I added that to this story because it would sound so much better. It was the only way it'd be believable that I would feel I had no choice but to take him away, hide him to protect him from more trauma in his life.

Thankfully, the cops never demanded to see the PET scans; they just took my word for it. I have to admit that I was a little nervous about that part. Not that I wouldn't have come up with a way to explain it away, of course. I always did, one way or another.

Was I convincing as Shane's caring mom in my story? I hope I was. I really went all into my role. You know, method acting, the kind I learned at the Lee Strasberg Institute. I used method acting to become sweet Jennifer, who had devoted her life to her fucked-up son. Most of the time, I truly *was* this annoying Jennifer. Man, did I hate myself!

I absolutely hate overbearing, crunchy, neurotic moms like I played all that time. I was so glad I could be myself now, especially with Shane. Well, most of the time. Whenever people were around, I acted like *nice* Jennifer. Yuck.

Anyway, he finally knows why he's in jail, why he'll be rotting in jail until he kills himself or another kid kills him. He has to pay for killing Peter. He finally understands that's what this was all about.

To be honest, I had a moment of weakness. Toward the end of our trip, I was thinking about making him my new partner, training him to become a killer. Being on the lam, it wasn't like he'd have a choice but to do what I wanted him to do anyway. Obviously, I did *not* have an affair with that fat, old pig, also known as Dr. Jonathan Wilkins. He was a terrible psychologist. Seriously. He had no idea who I really was. The affair was just a lie to throw off Shane, and so was the story about the patient who had raped and killed his ex-wife. I can't believe Shane bought that stupid story even for one second. I mean, how the hell would I know the size of that guy's *shoes?* How would I have gotten a hold of his watch?

Unbelievable.

Anyway, when Shane brought that old bag to our room, I had no choice but to kill her and make it seem like Shane had done it. That went very easily, thank God, especially considering that I had taken the precaution to shut down those nasty little cameras the day before. Having been at The Shithole before—that's what Peter and I liked to call it back in the day—I knew exactly how those cameras worked. All that was needed to make them inoperable was to cut the cords behind them. So I did. No one had been around to see which one of us had pushed her down the stairs, never mind snapped her neck when she had refused to die. The old bitch must have had real bad osteoporosis because it had taken me zero effort to break her neck. It had felt like a bird's.

You probably wonder how come I'm not in jail for harboring a criminal. Well, I knew it was likely I could strike a deal with the prosecutor in exchange for witnessing against my son. And it had turned out, I could. When I told them I was willing to confess that I had seen Shane return home at four in the morning the night Dr. Wilkins had been killed, my lawyer told me we would accept nothing less than me serving no time at all in exchange for that testimony.

Of course they had agreed.

People can be so naïve.

I'm going to have a glass of wine now. I used to not be able to handle alcohol. I drank in secret in the years after Peter's death as a way to cope with all the grief. Hardly anyone knew about my excessive drinking habits. Only my mom and my son. When I realized I could channel my grief into planning my revenge against my bastard son, I stopped drinking. I stopped feeling the need to get drunk out of my mind and only had a drink every now and then.

I can enjoy a glass of wine just like any other normal person now.

I'll be reading through my finished screenplay as I drink my wine. I'll pause and pore over the part I added when nice Jennifer learned that an anonymous person had called in a tip about having seen someone who looked just like Shane outside Dr. Wilkins's apartment building. That person was me. By now, you've gotten that already, right? *I* was the person calling the cops, leaving that tip. I had to make it extra urgent for us to run away.

Obviously, the movie ends with me becoming all depressed after I realize I can't save my son, not with me having set him up all along. It ends when I realize I have to do the right thing, turn him in to the authorities before he can do more harm in the world. Everything besides the lies I told Shane are true in the story. They happened just like I told you. Shane did kill our cat. But he wasn't stabbing it as viciously as I described it in the beginning of this story. The cat wasn't half decapitated. I just added that because I thought it would make for a great opening. Which it did, right? And the cat did have rabies. Shane never tossed it out in some creek. He buried it in the backyard and even put a wooden cross on the grave. I was curious to find out if it had been as rabid as it had looked from outside the living room, so I had it dug up and checked. It definitely had rabies.

Oh, and I also made up that he confessed to killing his father on purpose. Since the little shit refuses to admit the truth to me, I had no choice but to make it up.

Anyway, it's a brilliant, brilliant story. Not only will it make me rich, but also famous for sure. Even better, it will, as always, give me the last laugh. I hope you'll enjoy it as much as I enjoyed writing it.

Cheers,

Jennifer

EPILOGUE

I t's 2015 now and I have been in juvy for two years, almost exactly to the day. I know that Mom is crazy, crazy for real. So crazy that she thinks I killed Dad *on purpose.* I didn't kill him on purpose. It was all an accident.

But she refuses to believe me, and this is why I am in jail now. She needed me to pay for what I had done to her husband, my dad. I have come to the conclusion that my mom, and probably my dad too, is a psychopath of the worst kind. She can fool literally *anyone.* She sure had me fooled for the longest time. But I'm older now, older and nowhere near as naïve as I used to be.

She says that she's surprised that I'm still alive. That I haven't tried to hang myself or something. That none of the other kids here have tried to kill me. She doesn't realize that I'm not the dumb kid she was used to. The kid she could fool so easily. I have learned how to survive in juvy. It took me only a few months of bad beatings to realize that I needed to be the one in charge, not the one everyone pushed around. It took three guys gang raping me one night for me to wake up and start to fight for my life. I refused to be a victim anymore. So I started to work out and align myself with two beefy guys who are actually good people. They watched my back. And then, when I turned fourteen a little over a year ago, I started to grow. A lot. Now, at fifteen, I'm six foot two and very muscular.

I'm getting out of here in less than three years if I can behave as well as I've done so far. And I think I can. I know the ropes now. I'm the one who calls the shots in here. No one messes with me anymore.

I'll make it till I'm eighteen and free again. And then I'll come after you, Mommy Dearest. I'll make *you* pay. We'll see who gets the last laugh in the end.

AFTERWORD

Thank you for reading BORN EVIL. If you want to receive notices about my book releases, click HERE to join my mailing list. Word-of-mouth is crucial for any author to succeed. If you enjoyed this story, please review it at your vendor. Even if it's just a sentence or two.

TRUE EVIL, THE SEQUEL, IS NOW AVAILABLE!

ALSO BY JULIA DEREK

The Traitor

The Scientist

DUPLICITY (Prequel to the Girl Undercover Series)

Duplicity

THE SMILEY KILLER (Companion book to the Girl Undercover Series)

The Smiley Killer

The Celeste Jones Paranormal Mystery Series (Cozy mysteries)

Haunted Hardbodies

Spooky Hardbodies

Ghostly Hardbodies

The Evil Trilogy (Psychological Thriller)

Born Evil

True Evil

Printed in Great Britain
by Amazon